Stories of Azoria
Part 1

Alex O.Harb

Stories of Azoria. Part 1
Copyright © 2025 by Alex O. Harb
All rights reserved.

The story, all names, characters, and incidents portrayed in this production are fictitious.

Book Cover by Alex O. Harb
Illustrations by GetCovers.com, Alex O. Harb
Second edition 2025

ISBN 979-8-9992133-4-1 (paperback)
ISBN 979-8-9992133-3-4 (ebook)

ALEX O. HARB

RESONANCE
OF
SILENCE

RESONANCE OF SILENCE

Davin Teller thought he was the unluckiest man alive. He had never succeeded at anything he tried. Maybe it had something to do with the fact that he was a fraud. He started a mineral trading company without a single mine or contract. He launched a travel company with bright, colorful posters – but not one deal with an actual agency. He sold apartments on nonexistent worlds and played in a "very popular" music band that toured from nowhere to even less.

Every time he failed, he blamed someone else – stupid customers, greedy partners, even the unfair judge. Of course, he knew how to play guitar – he'd taken a two-week holo course. And all his other ventures? Absolutely real. Plenty of people made a living as middlemen, and Davin just needed a little more time to subcontract the services he'd already been paid for.

Now, sitting in the cramped escape pod as it hurtled through the unfamiliar atmosphere, Davin had plenty of time to reflect on how the universe – and everything in it – had conspired against him once again.

His musical "talents" had been his latest attempt to improve his circumstances. The prison shuttle guards had allowed inmates to form an impromptu band during recreation hours. Davin immediately appointed himself lead guitarist and vocalist, proudly claiming years of concert experience. He even tried to print a tuning fork for "perfect musical pitch" using the rec room's 3D printer.

The resulting fork emitted an ugly, wailing tone that had nothing to do with music. Davin kept it anyway – either as a souvenir or for some future scheme.

Three chords and an excruciating rendition of *Nebula Heart* later, his fellow inmates made their feelings known with a barrage of food remnants and a chorus of boos.

"Uncultured criminals," Davin muttered, flicking a glob of synthetic protein off his prison jumpsuit.

He'd been in the restroom, wondering if the tuning fork might double as a cleaning tool when the alarms began to wail. The shuttle's engines had suffered a catastrophic failure – just one more cruel coincidence in his long, unlucky streak.

In the ensuing chaos, Davin had hesitated too long. By the time he reached the evacuation bay, the main pod – the one with actual navigation systems, emergency supplies, and trained personnel – was already detaching. He caught a final glimpse of the guards and prisoners strapped safely inside as it launched toward the planet below.

Left with no choice, he scrambled into the only thing left: a single-occupant emergency pod with minimal systems and no pilot interface to speak of. The kind meant for unconscious passengers. The kind no one was supposed to need.

The pod vibrated violently as it pierced the upper atmosphere of the planet – Azoria, as the nav screen flickered before it went dark. Through the tiny viewport, he watched the main escape pod descend into a dense, swirling layer of dark clouds that wrapped the entire planet.

His own pod, however, veered toward a cluster of... floating platforms? Tourist attractions, most likely – hovering just above the storm line, designed for aesthetics and brochure photography.

The kind of thing he might have featured in one of his own travel scams.

"Someone spent a lot of credits and effort building these," he said aloud to the empty pod. "Must be one hell of a luxury resort."

The pod gave a final shudder before crashing unceremoniously onto the surface of the floating island. The impact wasn't as bad as Davin had feared – some part of the automatic landing system must have still been online.

When the ringing in his ears faded, he pulled himself upright and inspected the control panel. Dead. Not a single light. Not even emergency power. He pressed the beacon button repeatedly, thumped the console with his fist, and finally tried the age-old fix: off, then on again. Nothing.

"No matter," he muttered. "The shuttle must have sent a distress signal. Rescue ships are probably already en route."

He unlatched the pod's hatch and shoved it open. A rush of fresh air swept in, carrying scents of vegetation and damp soil. Davin stepped out and turned slowly, taking in his new surroundings.

The floating island was far larger than it had looked from above – maybe a few square miles of rocky terrain, scattered with stunted trees and sparse undergrowth. The breeze stirred the foliage beneath a pale sky. Off in the distance, other islands hung motionless in the open air – some large, some no more than specks. All impossibly suspended.

A low rumble broke his thoughts. He turned, half-expecting to see the shining hull of a Federation rescue vessel.

Instead, a massive zeppelin drifted into view. It looked like something out of a museum: steam puffed from unseen valves as it glided between two floating isles, canvas sails catching the wind, wooden hull gleaming in the diffuse light. There were no holographic billboards, no logos. Just bare, antique elegance.

Davin sank down onto a nearby rock, wincing as the tuning fork – or "resonator," as he preferred to call it – dug into his thigh through his jumpsuit pocket. He looked up at the gathering clouds and sighed.

"Just my luck," he muttered. "Hundreds of planets in colonized space, and I crash on the one with anti-gravity islands and steaming balloon rides. Someone in Rescue Coordination is definitely going to hear about this."

———

A dozen men and women made up the crew of the trading zeppelin *Merciful Breeze*, all dressed in layered clothing of muted browns and grays. They stared openly at Davin's bright orange prison jumpsuit as he was escorted to the captain's cabin.

"I am Hobart, master of this vessel," said the bearded man who had first spotted him. He was shorter than Davin had anticipated, with calloused hands and eyes the color of weathered copper. "You come from the farthest realms of the Drift Lords? Your craft fell from the heavens themselves?"

"I need to contact Federation Emergency Services immediately," Davin replied, adopting his most authoritative tone. "I'm a government consultant on an urgent mission."

The lie came as naturally as breathing. In Davin's experience, claiming to be someone important was the fastest way to receive preferential treatment. The metal resonator sat heavily in his pocket – his only possession, but not his only asset. Reinvention was his true talent.

Hobart's brow furrowed. "Fed-er-a-tion?" he echoed, awkwardly shaping the word. "I know not this term."

"My governmental organization," Davin said, slowing his speech. "I need access to our comm hub."

"Comm… hub?" Hobart repeated, then shook his head. "These words have no meaning, stranger."

It took Davin nearly an hour to spot the pattern – and when he did, it left a cold knot in his gut. These people understood basic Federation Standard remarkably well, but words like spaceship, radio, shuttle, and transmission earned only blank stares or puzzled attempts at repetition.

It was as if the very concept of technology beyond steam power had vanished from their vocabulary.

"We journey to Silence Drift," Captain Hobart said at last. "The capital of the Silent Principality. Perhaps someone there can help you find your… people."

"What sort of communication technology do you have?" Davin asked. "Surely you must have some way to contact other… vessels."

Hobart exchanged a glance with the first mate.

"Signal flags for short distances," she said. "Messenger birds for urgent matters. The speaking trumpets, when vessels draw alongside."

Davin blinked. "No radio? No ansible communications? Not even a basic wave transmitter?"

The silence was answer enough. The blank stares told him everything.

———

The zeppelin continued its trading run to two more floating islands before setting a course for the capital.

Davin spent the journey entertaining the crew with elaborate tales of his importance in the Federation Diplomatic Corps and his daring exploits on distant worlds. The crew listened with fascination – though he noticed they seemed far more impressed by his descriptions of oceans than by anything involving space travel or advanced technology.

By the third day, Davin had pieced together a rough understanding of the world he had landed in. The Silent Principality was one of several nations scattered across the floating landmasses suspended above a vast planetary phenomenon known only as The Storm.

The Storm enveloped the entire planet and seemed to halt technological progress through persistent electromagnetic interference.

Their destination, the Principality, had been founded on devotion to something called the Sacred Stillness – a belief that perfect silence enables perfect communion with the divine.

Silence Drift stretched across a floating landmass larger than any Davin had seen so far. Structures of stone and wood rose in concentric rings around a massive central complex. Unlike the sleek towers of Federation cities, the skyline here was defined by squat, circular towers with peculiar acoustic-dampening panels clearly visible even from a distance.

"The Chambers of Quietude," Captain Hobart explained in a reverent whisper. "Where the faithful gather for Silent Prayer. Perhaps you'll find work there. Or shelter."

With that, Davin stepped off the zeppelin and onto the city of Silence Drift.

The city's residents paced slowly, as if deliberately meant to blend into the background. Thick carpets, laid over cobblestone streets, muffled their footsteps. Conversations were carried out in hushed tones, barely audible above the gentle hiss of steam engines and the soft flutter of trading banners.

Davin soon discovered that his orange prison jumpsuit, crisp Federation accent, and total ignorance of local customs didn't mark him as an envoy – they made him a spectacle. His attempts to grift even a few coins of local currency ended in failure.

"I can read your fortune in the vibrations of your voice," he once offered to a noblewoman. She promptly summoned the Silencers – local law enforcement, who didn't bother arresting him. They simply shushed him away, sternly warning him not to "disturb the peace."

After two days of increasingly desperate efforts to gain a foothold, Davin found himself hungry, penniless, and sleeping in the shadow of the Grand Chamber of Quietude.

It was there that he learned of the Feeding of the Faithful.

"The Church feeds the faithful after morning contemplation," an elderly man whispered. "Even outsiders. But you must observe the full Hour of Silence."

Hunger proved to be a powerful motivator.

The next morning, Davin joined a line of the city's destitute as they filed into the Grand Chamber.

The interior was stranger than anything he'd imagined – every surface coated with angled acoustic panels, soft textures, and sound-dampening fabrics. The ceiling arched high overhead like the inside of an enormous eggshell. Shallow pools of water lined the perimeter walls, reflecting the silence in perfect stillness.

A priest in gray robes raised a hand for silence. Then, with great ceremony, he turned the ornate water clock in the center of the chamber.

For the next hour, two hundred people sat in complete stillness as water dripped rhythmically from one glass bulb to another.

It was, without question, the most excruciating hour of Davin's life. Worse than his trial. Worse than the Nebula Heart performance. He spent it plotting his next move.

The midday meal that followed – thin gruel with bread – barely seemed worth the effort. But it kept him alive.

Two days of whispered prayers, stiff stone corners, and flavorless porridge dulled Davin's pride and sharpened his instincts. On the third morning, as he watched a street preacher draw a crowd (and a modest pile of donations) with hushed sermons on the virtues of silence, inspiration struck.

That evening, Davin absorbed as much of the Church's doctrine as he could from borrowed texts, whispered conversations, and sheer improvisation.

The next morning, he dragged a wooden crate into the market square, climbed atop it, and raised his voice far louder than was considered decent.

"People of Silence Drift!" he called, projecting with deliberate volume. "You have been misled!"

The crowd froze. A dozen horrified faces turned toward him in unified disbelief. Encouraged, Davin pressed on.

"Silence is not the path to divinity! It is sound – the *Resonant Harmony* – that brings true communion!"

He pulled the metal tuning fork from his pocket and raised it high, like a relic of holy power. "I am a prophet from beyond the upper mists! The celestial beings have shown me: silence is the absence of truth. Divinity lies in perfect acoustic balance!"

A small crowd formed – some curious, some scandalized. Davin continued his sermon, blending pseudo-scientific jargon with vague theological claims, offering "acoustic blessings" in exchange for whispered prayers and loose coins.

For nearly twenty minutes, it worked. He even had a few believers.

Then a sharp voice hissed through the murmuring crowd.

"Silence breaker!"

A temple guard pointed directly at him. "Blasphemer!"

The crowd's curiosity turned to anger.

Davin snatched the coins and bolted, weaving through the streets with an angry mob at his heels. Desperate, he ducked into the Grand Chamber of Quietude, hoping to lose them among the maze of prayer panels.

The vast chamber was nearly empty – only a few priests lingered, preparing for the midday service. Davin darted between the sound-dampening panels, heart pounding. The voices of his pursuers echoed faintly behind him, growing louder.

Then, as he turned a corner, his grip faltered. The tuning fork slipped from his sweaty hand and struck the polished stone floor with a high-pitched wail. Davin froze.

The tone did not fade.

Instead, it grew – reflected, reinforced, and amplified by the chamber's precisely angled acoustic panels. The sound rippled outward, a pure note resonating in waves.

The mob halted in the doorway, their anger forgotten as the tone washed over them. The priests stood frozen, their expressions a mixture of awe and fear.

For nearly a minute, the resonance filled the chamber – growing neither louder nor softer, but steady and perfect, vibrating within the bones of everyone present.

When it finally faded, silence returned with a pressure that felt almost sacred.

One of the pursuers, an old man with trembling hands, stepped forward.

"The *Resonant Harmony*," he whispered, dropping to his knees. "How is this possible? The Chamber has never produced a sound."

Davin looked from the man to the fork on the floor, then back to the crowd now watching him, not with fury but with reverence.

In that crystalline moment, he understood exactly what had happened: the architecture, the acoustic math, the coincidental pitch of the fork. A perfect accident, interpreted as a miracle by people with no framework for what they had seen.

His luck had finally changed.

"Perhaps," he said gravely, lifting the fork from the floor and raising it with slow ceremony, "silence is merely the canvas upon which divine harmony is painted."

———

Six months after his arrival, as Davin presided over a ceremony honoring his "divine revelation," Federation rescue finally arrived – part of a routine search pattern for a prison shuttle crash.

They never found the main pod – the Storm's electromagnetic interference made detailed scans and close-range searches impossible. What they did find was the crash site of the secondary pod, stranded on a remote floating island, its surface overgrown and windswept. There was no trace of inmate #45773.

The squadron commander filed a terse report: *Crew and inmates are presumed deceased. Case closed.*

Davin – now known as The Prophet – never knew of it. He was too busy leading his congregation in perfect harmony, their voices rising as one to embrace the divine, not in silence but in sound.

Some forms of luck, it seemed, weren't so bad after all.

ALEX O. HARB

THE
PLAN
OF
DARKNESS

THE PLAN OF DARKNESS

Most of all, Malik Dunn was afraid of digging too deep and falling through the bottom of the rock. In the mine, he always tried to move forward, not down – doubling back often to check that his tunnel wasn't dipping lower than the others.

He raised his lantern. The yellow light flickered, catching a speck of bluish mineral in the stone. He'd been chipping away at this section of the High Eastern Tunnel for three weeks with nothing to show for it. But now, finally, luck had shown its face.

The smart thing – the thing his supervisor would say – was to report it right away.

But something else had been whispering to him lately. A feeling. A voice. *Take it.*

His fingers moved before he really thought about it. The rock was cool and smooth. Glassy. His heart thumped. This wasn't just a streak – it was a proper find. Maybe enough to pay rent for months.

He glanced over his shoulder. The other miners were way back, their picks still echoing down the tunnel. No one was watching.

He swapped in his smaller pick, the one for careful work, and chipped loose a chunk the size of his palm. It floated – barely – a little lift that made his stomach jump. Malik shoved it into the iron sample box fast.

Then he pulled out the measuring rod like the rules said, checked the size of the vein, and yelled back.

"Found somethin'!"

Foreman Jackson's voice came from deeper in the tunnel. "You got a hit, Dunn?"

Malik nodded as the man approached. "Yeah. Blue-vein. Not huge."

Jackson looked and gave a small nod. "Good one. You'll get a premium."

"Thanks. I could use it."

Hourly pay didn't go far. But floatstone – Rational Element, the fancy name – could mean the difference between scraping by and living a little better. The Kingdom of Azurath needed every bit of it. It was how the islands stayed up. How the skyships flew.

Jackson clapped him on the shoulder. "Carry on. I'll send Morris to assist."

As the foreman walked off, Malik's hand went to his pocket. The iron box felt warm. Or maybe that was just him.

You need more, the voice said again, quiet but sharp.

He'd taken nothing before. Not really. Never even thought about it.

But right now, with the stone in his pocket and no one watching, he didn't feel bad. He just felt… like he needed more.

———

Malik sat on the edge of his bed. The floatstone hovered above the table.

Every night, it was the same: open the box, watch it float, then go to sleep and wake from yet another nightmare. Watching the floatstone made it easier. It calmed him.

The stone gave off a faint blue light in the dark. It made his fingers look strange, almost ghostly.

He knew every part of it now – the tiny copper fleck at the base, the sharp edge near one side, the thin lines in the crystal like cracks in glass.

Since that first day, he'd found three more veins. Real ones. Reported them, got his premiums.

But they didn't feel right. None of them felt like this one.

"Show me how to find more," he whispered.

Find the pure ones, the voice said. *The truth is in the perfect form.*

At first, it had just been a feeling. Like a gut hunch. Lately, it was more.

A real voice. Always there, just behind his thoughts.

He called it the Darkness. It lived in the corners of his mind where the light didn't reach.

Blue dust stuck under his nails. He rubbed at it. "Just dust," he muttered.

The door lock clicked. Malik quickly covered the floatstone with a scrap cloth.

Lisha stepped in, her canteen smock spotted with grease and broth.

"Thought your shift started early?"

"Couldn't sleep."

She took off the smock and dropped it on the hook, then sat beside him.

"Jackson's wife says you've been findin' more floatstone."

"Been lucky," he said.

She leaned against his shoulder. "Maybe we can get a place with a window."

He nodded. It was a nice thought. But his mind was already drifting – thinking about the tunnels, about the other veins, about how much more he could take before someone noticed.

You've taken the first step, the voice whispered.

That night, he dreamed of falling again – down through the clouds, toward the roaring Storm.

But he didn't see the other fall. The slow one. Inwards.

———

"The union needs someone who knows what it's like down there in the tunnels," said Councilor Ellis Nask, looking Malik straight in the eye. "Someone the boys trust. That's you, Dunn."

He nodded slow, heart beating faster than he liked.

A year ago, he'd been just another miner. Quiet. Kept his head down. Now he was the one they came to when something wasn't right. When the foremen tried to cut rest breaks, he was the one who stood up and said no. When the vents failed last month and the boss wanted to keep digging, Malik shut the whole level down until it got fixed.

The blue stains on his fingers had darkened, but it was common for the floatstone miners. No one asked.

"I'd be honored," he said. "But I never led nothin'."

Nask leaned forward. "You led just fine when the vent went bad. Entire crew could've been gassed. They follow you, Dunn."

He wasn't wrong.

20

He had been speaking up more lately. Reading, too – union rules, old pamphlets, legal documents he'd once thought were only for politicians and lawyers. Now they made sense. He had studied obsessively – politics, rhetoric, history, law. Enough to pass reforms no one expected from a miner, to write proposals even senior ministers couldn't easily reject. What had once been confusion was now strategy. He wasn't becoming smarter or getting some hidden knowledge from the Darkness, but rather a push to learn, to speak, to advance. He knew how to speak so people listened – and how to write so they couldn't say no. The voice in his head kept pushing. Telling him what mattered. Where to look. What to say.

The nightmares still came. Burning cities. Stones falling from the sky. But they didn't matter. Not when he had a purpose now.

That night, he stepped into the apartment and froze. Lisha was at the table. His box was open. Seven floatstone pieces, each one fixed to a weighted base. Each one burned into his memory.

"What is this?" she asked, quiet and sharp.

His mouth went dry. "I can explain–"

"You stealin' from the mine?" She stood, eyes wide. "You know what they'll do if they find this?"

"I ain't–" He stopped. Even now, his hands twitched toward the box.

She wants to take it from you, the voice said. *It's yours.*

"We takin' it back," Lisha said. "You'll tell 'em you was holdin' samples. Maybe they'll let it slide."

"No." It came out hard, too fast.

"Yes," she snapped. "This ain't right, Malik. Look at your hands!"

She grabbed his wrist and pulled off the glove. The blue had spread – fingers, palms, halfway to the wrist.

Malik yanked his hand back.

"You don't get it," he said, voice tight. "This is just the start. I got offered union leadership."

Lisha stared at him. "It's changin' you. This ain't the man I knew. He was happy enough with what he had."

"Happy enough?" Malik snapped. "You said maybe one day we'd get a place with a window. That was your big dream."

She flinched. "That ain't fair," she whispered.

"You know what ain't fair?" he growled, stepping closer. "Men breakin' their backs while the Kingdom floats off our sweat. Someone's gotta speak up. Someone like me."

Lisha's eyes hardened. "I'm turnin' these in. Tomorrow."

Stop her, the voice hissed. *She'll take it all.*

Something snapped.

His hand moved before he thought. The slap rang out. Lisha staggered back, clutching her face, her eyes wide and wet.

Malik froze. He couldn't move. Couldn't look away from what he'd done. Heat rushed through him. "Lisha, I–"

But she was already pulling her smock from the hook, stuffing a few clothes into her old satchel, tears streaming down her cheeks.

"You're sick, Malik," she said without looking at him. "And I can't help you if you won't help yourself."

The door slammed behind her. Malik stood there, frozen.

He should've run after her. Should've said something.

Instead, his feet took him to the box. His hands – still shaking – lifted the lid.

He checked each piece. Slowly. Carefully. One by one.

None were broken.

His fingers trembled. Not from guilt. Not exactly.

She would've held you back, the Darkness said. *You need to find the pure ones.*

Malik pressed his palms to his temples, squeezing his eyes shut. "What am I turnin' into?"

Something necessary, came the answer. *This is just the start.*

And deep down, Malik knew it was right.

He hid the minerals and when the search came and found nothing, told them with a straight face that Lisha was making it up to punish him after their break up.

"Looks like the stone's cracking under strain," Malik said, tapping the readout with a callused finger.

The other apprentices leaned in, frowning. Master Renhald adjusted his spectacles.

"Go on," the old man said. "What does that tell you?"

Malik shifted the clamp on the floatstone, making sure the weighted base held it steady.

"If the fractures go past this point," he pointed to a sharp dip in the graph, "the lift becomes unstable. Could push too hard or fail altogether."

Renhald gave a slow nod. "Dangerous in a crafted piece."

"Especially in airship stabilizers or float rings," Malik said.

He caught one of the others glancing sideways at him.

Five years ago, they wouldn't have believed he'd end up here – out of the mines, out of the union office, standing in a workshop instead. But he'd earned it. Every hour studying. Every night grinding numbers until the voice in his head stopped whispering long enough to let him sleep.

And still, it wasn't enough. Not yet.

Master Renhald peered through his lenses. "You've been digging through the old Guild records."

"Every night," Malik said.

The Darkness wouldn't let him stop. It needed him to know – everything about floatstone, about lift, about failure. He slept maybe two hours at a time now. Just enough to keep going. Just enough to dream.

And the dreams were changing: waves swallowing cities, flaming stones crashing from the sky. And always – always – the fall.

Later that night, in his cramped quarters, Malik sat under the lamplight and rolled up his sleeves. The blue had climbed past his wrists, halfway up his arms now. He wore long sleeves, even in the heat. The craving never left him. It scratched at the edge of his thoughts, a constant need – not for food or comfort, but for something purer, deeper, unseen.

The Darkness had given that need a name.

The seedpod, it whispered. *You have to find it. The pure source. The beginning of the beginning.*

Malik flexed his stained fingers, palms pulsing faint blue in the lamplight. "I don't even know what that is," he muttered.

The Darkness didn't answer. It didn't have to.

A knock at the door pulled him out of thought.

One of the younger apprentices stood outside, wringing his hands. "Sorry, Master Dunn. There's someone here to see you. Says it's urgent."

Malik followed him through the quiet halls. In the front chamber, a man in a worn coat waited beneath the flickering lanterns. Malik recognized him – one of the old union messengers, now working as a courier for the guilds.

"Message from Senior Blacksmith Carter," the man said, handing over a folded slip of paper. "Said it had to get to you tonight."

Malik broke the seal.

You're not alone. I've seen what's happening to your hands. Most of us get the stains – but few are driven like you are. There's a name for it: blue fever. My grandfather had it. Affects the mind. Makes you hear things. See things. Meet me at The Broken Anvil tomorrow. I know someone who might help. – C

Malik lowered the note, his fingers cold.

Blue fever.

The old stories from the mines had a name here too. He'd heard the whispers – of craftsmen who vanished after chasing floatstone across the skies. Of artists who claimed the stone spoke to them. Of visions. Of craving.

He looked down at his hands.

The blue wasn't fading. It was spreading.

He means to stop you, the voice whispered. *He fears what you're becoming.*

"No," Malik muttered. "He wants to help."

The courier gave him a sideways glance but said nothing.

They all want to hold you back. Just like Lisha did.

Her face flashed through his mind – tear-streaked, stunned, backing away.

How many times had he wondered where she'd gone? If she'd found someone else. Someone with clean hands. Someone without a voice inside his head.

His hands trembled as he folded the letter. "Tell Carter I'll be there."

But even as the words left his mouth, his gut twisted. He wasn't going. He already knew.

The voice – his quiet companion, his shadow – had grown louder. Sharper. Closer.

That night, he dreamed again.

A perfect sphere of floatstone hovered before him, pulsing with blue light. Bigger than any sample he'd ever held. Alive somehow. It thrummed like a heartbeat – like the pulse of the world itself.

He reached for it.

And when his fingers brushed the surface, he heard the voice – not as a whisper, but as something vast and certain.

Soon, it said. *Soon you will understand the Plan.*

Malik never went to the meeting.

Instead, he buried himself in his work, chasing that perfect sphere from his dreams – something more than fragments. Something vast. Something the voice called a seedpod.

The Parliament chamber buzzed with raised voices and shuffling papers, the golden emblems of Azurath glinting under the dome lights. Malik sat stiffly in his assigned seat, the blue-and-gold sash of the Mining District draped across his chest. At thirty-five, he had made it – out of the tunnels, past the guild halls, and into the

Kingdom's highest chamber. What once felt impossible now hung on his shoulders like armor.

"The honorable representative from the Mining District has the floor," the chamber secretary announced.

Malik rose, his gloved hands gripping the podium. The gloves hid what they always had – fingers permanently stained blue, the mark creeping past his elbows now, reaching his neck. He wore high collars these days. Most would ignore it anyway – floatstone commonly caused such discoloration. Ten years had passed since someone first called it "blue fever." He had never followed up. Never wanted to know for sure.

Ten years of restless sleep, of voices in the dark. The Darkness no longer whispered. It spoke clearly now, with purpose and weight.

The Plan is close, it had said that morning. *The world must be made ready.*

"Esteemed colleagues," he began, his voice carrying the confidence that had won him his seat. "The proposed floatstone quotas would cripple our ability to maintain essential infrastructure. We must consider the practical implications for our floating communities."

As he spoke, part of him still marveled at the transformation. The simple miner who once stumbled through reports in front of foremen now addressed Parliament with an eloquence that commanded silence. He excelled in politics, rhetoric, history, and law – disciplines he'd once viewed as distant, now second nature. To most, he appeared eccentric but brilliant – the man whose strange habits were overlooked for the sake of his insight. Nobody suspected the truth: that something lived inside his mind, whispering guidance, feeding him visions of ruin and renewal.

Three years into his parliamentary term, Malik had become known for his unwavering defense of the mining guilds and for proposing reforms that, while unorthodox, often worked. In public, he was driven and effective. In private, the obsession ruled him. The Darkness urged him to search for purer and rarer forms of floatstone. It showed him the fragments of a raging storm – visions threaded through his dreams, speaking of collapse and rebirth.

After one particularly bitter session, Malik drifted through the market district. His formal jacket open, his boots scraping cobblestone. He wasn't sure why he'd come – only that something had pulled him there, quiet and insistent, like a tug behind the eyes.

As he walked, he paused near a storefront, staring at his reflection in the glass. His fine clothes couldn't hide the truth. For all his achievements, his life was empty, his house echoed with silence. No Lisha. No friends waiting. The colleagues who admired his mind, kept their distance from the man himself. He'd worked himself to exhaustion for years, climbed from the mines to Parliament – and for what? A voice that was not his own, driving him toward goals he didn't understand.

What had he gained, really? Power? Respect? These things seemed empty now. He couldn't even remember the last time he'd truly laughed. The obsession had consumed everything.

And yet, he wouldn't stop. Couldn't stop.

"You there," Malik called, spotting a thin man in weather-stained traveling gear unpacking odd artifacts onto a market stall. Bronze trinkets, bird-bone flutes, bits of shaped stone – clearly tribal wares. "You trade with the Heights tribes, don't you?"

The man looked up, eyes sharp with appraisal. "When the wind's not trying to kill me. Why?"

"I'm paying for the info on tribal floatstone sources," Malik said, keeping his tone even. "Anything you know of purer deposits at higher altitudes."

The trader raised an eyebrow. "Guild business?"

"Personal interest," Malik replied, placing several polished high-value coins on the counter.

Ask him about the seedheart, the Darkness commanded.

"Ever heard of a seedheart?" Malik asked, watching the trader's face.

The man's expression flickered – first surprise, then something more cautious. "Where'd you hear that name?"

"Around," Malik said, keeping it vague. "Is it important?"

The trader pocketed the coins and leaned in. His voice dropped a notch. "There are stories, mostly from the Heights tribes. They talk about islands with perfect cores – floatstone that never weathers, never fades. They call them seedhearts. Supposedly, those islands float higher than any others. Out of reach."

Yes! The Darkness surged inside Malik's skull, a thrill like static cracking behind his eyes. *That's it! The seedpod!*

"Do you know where they are?" Malik asked, gripping the edge of the stall to keep his hands from shaking. He tried to sound calm, but the pressure inside him was building fast. The Darkness pressed closer, trembling with urgency.

The trader shrugged. "The tribes guard that kind of knowledge closely. But there's a rumor – one speaks of an island far to the north, past the Crimson Drifts. So high it's always frozen. Covered in ice year-round."

The key to the Plan! the Darkness exulted. *You must find it.*

"I need maps," Malik said, his voice rising with sudden urgency. "Tribal paths, navigation charts, anything that could point me to that island."

The trader gave a nervous laugh. "Those'd cost more than a few coins, friend. And even then, it's not like you can walk into a guild hall and ask for maps of myth."

"Name your price," Malik snapped, leaning forward. "Whatever it is – I can meet it."

Get everything from him, the Darkness urged. *You need the seedpod!*

The trader instinctively took a step back. Something in Malik's eyes – too intense, too hungry – had changed the air between them.

"Look," the man said, holding up a hand, "I don't have what you want. It's just a story. I heard it in a campfire circle, nothing more."

"You're lying," Malik growled, the Darkness swelling inside him. Before he could stop himself, he had grabbed the trader by the collar, lifting the smaller man nearly off his feet. "Tell me what you know!"

The market fell into sudden silence. Stalls stilled. Conversations stopped. People turned to stare at the well-dressed guildsman manhandling a traveling trader. Malik barely registered them. The Darkness had surged forward, drowning out caution and reason.

"Please," the trader gasped, face reddening. "I know nothing else!"

Something warm ran across Malik's knuckles. He looked down. Blood from the trader's nose dripped onto his fine guild robe, streaking the fabric with crimson. The sight snapped something loose. The pressure receded, and Malik let go abruptly.

Return! the Darkness hissed. *You need that information!*

But Malik was already backing away, heart pounding, sick with the weight of what he'd just done. The crowd was shifting, parting. Market guards were pushing through, drawn by the commotion.

"This isn't over," he muttered – not to the trader, but to himself. Then he turned and slipped into the crowd, the voice in his head heavy with disappointment.

That night, alone in his chamber, he stared at his reflection in a polished metal disc. The face that looked back was hardly recognizable as the simple miner who had once dreamed only of a room with a window. For a moment, he wondered what Lisha would think if she could see him now – parliamentary robes, articulate speech, and the haunted look of a man possessed.

The voice spoke to him with greater clarity than ever before.

You have wasted enough time, it said. *The seedpod is the key to everything. To the Plan.*

"What is this Plan you keep mentioning?" Malik asked aloud, no longer caring if others might hear him talking to himself. He was past such concerns.

Renewal, the Darkness replied. *The floating lands must return to the sea. The cycle must complete.*

Malik shuddered. "Return to the sea? You mean… fall? That would kill millions."

Billions will arise. A new world must be born. As intended.

"I don't understand," Malik whispered.

You will, the Darkness promised. *When you find the seedpod – everything will become clear. You are my instrument, Malik Dunn. You will help birth the new world.*

In that moment, something shifted within Malik. The last barrier between him and the Darkness crumbled, and he surrendered to the voice that had guided him for so long. If finding this seedheart would bring understanding and explain the nightmares and voices that haunted him for nearly twenty years, then that's what he would do.

Whatever the cost.

———

The zeppelin cut through the clouds, its gondola swaying gently beneath the massive gas envelope. Malik stood at the observation window, watching the Crimson Drifts recede behind them. At forty-five, his hair started graying at the temples, but his body remained strong, hardened by years in mines.

For seven years, he had devoted every resource, every connection, every coin to finding the seedheart island. His political career had been abandoned – his parliamentary seat lost after he began missing crucial votes. His guild position had been resigned, his reputation sacrificed in pursuit of what others dismissed as a delusion. But the Darkness had guided him, urging him to get tribal maps, bribe officials, assemble the expedition that would finally bring him to his destination.

As the zeppelin drifted through a bank of clouds, Malik felt a rare moment of clarity. Twenty-seven years had passed since he'd first touched that piece of floatstone in the mine. Nearly three decades chasing a voice that wasn't his own.

He leaned his forehead against the cool glass. What might his life have been if he'd never found that first sample? If he'd followed Lisha when she left? If he'd accepted help when Carter offered it? The questions gnawed at him.

He achieved things beyond anything the young miner could have imagined. But they'd never been his goals. His ambitions. They were stepping stones toward something else. Something the Darkness wanted.

Malik wondered what had become of Lisha. Had she found happiness? Had she thought of him in all these years? He imagined her living somewhere with that window she'd wanted, perhaps with children who would never know the miner with blue-stained hands who had once loved their mother.

"We'll reach the trading outpost by tomorrow morning," said the zeppelin captain, approaching from the control room. "I've confirmed your arrangement with the pilot who will take you to the Heights."

Malik nodded, not bothering to look at the man. "Good. Make sure my equipment is transferred properly."

"Sir, about the rest of the payment…"

"You'll receive it when we reach the outpost," Malik said firmly. "As agreed."

The captain hesitated. "If you don't mind my asking, what exactly are you hoping to find up there? Those tribal territories are notoriously dangerous, and beyond them–"

"That's my concern," Malik interrupted. "Yours is getting me to the trading outpost."

He asks too many questions, the Darkness said. *He suspects.*

After the captain returned to the control room, Malik removed his right glove, examining his blue-stained hand. The discoloration had spread up his arms years ago, eventually reaching his chest in a network of azure veins. He'd long since stopped caring who noticed.

So close now, the Darkness murmured, a rare note of excitement in its usually calm voice. *After all these years, the seedpod is within reach.*

Two days later, after a tense flight, they landed at a small trading outpost. As promised, a specialized aircraft waited, designed for the thin air and freezing temperatures of the highest altitudes. The trader who owned it eyed Malik nervously.

"You're sure about this?" the man asked as they completed the arrangements. "That island… the tribes avoid it except for their most sacred rituals. They say it's where the world began."

Where the world will begin again, the Darkness corrected, though only Malik could hear.

"I'm sure," Malik said firmly. "I'll manage."

The trader shrugged. "Your funeral. But at least take emergency supplies. If you crash up there, no one's coming to rescue you."

Malik paid the man his fee, making it clear their arrangement was concluded. "Wait two days. If I haven't returned, you can leave."

The trader looked uneasy. "Sir, you really shouldn't go alone—"

"This journey is mine to make," Malik said. The matter already decided.

The next morning, Malik boarded the specialized aircraft alone. It was built for extreme altitudes – thin air, freezing temperatures, minimal lift – but the controls were unlike those he had trained on. Before the expedition, he had scraped together what lessons he could, enough to understand the basics. Now, faced with an unfamiliar dashboard and a sky where every mistake could be fatal, he took a breath and began. His hands moved cautiously, hesitantly

– then with resolve. It wasn't precise, but it would fly. That was all he needed.

"There's no turning back," he thought.

There was never any turning back, the Darkness replied. *Not from the moment you first touched the mineral.*

The realization should have terrified him, but Malik felt only a strange calm as he started the engine. The craft shuddered, then lifted from the trading outpost's small landing pad. Within minutes, he was climbing higher; the air growing thinner; the temperature dropping rapidly. He approached the coordinates that had cost him his career, his reputation, and nearly two decades of his life.

Soon, said the Darkness, with what almost sounded like longing. *We're almost there.*

The island hung in the sky like a massive, jagged diamond, its surface glittering with ice. Malik circled it once, searching for a suitable landing place, the aircraft struggling in the thin air. The Darkness guided his hands on the controls, making adjustments he couldn't have made alone.

There, it directed, and Malik spotted a relatively flat expanse near what appeared to be a cave entrance.

The landing was rough; the craft skidding across the ice before coming to rest perilously close to the island's edge. Malik sat motionless for a moment, heart pounding. The landing gear was broken, and he wasn't sure he could fly it again.

The craft can remain here, the Darkness assured him. *You won't need it anymore.*

Stepping onto the island's surface, Malik felt a surge of emotion – a mixture of triumph, fear, and relief. After twenty years of searching, dreaming, and listening to the voices in his mind, he had finally reached his destination.

The cold was brutal, but he barely noticed. The Darkness drove him forward, toward the cave entrance he'd spotted from the air. As he approached, warmth seeped from within – impossible on an island sealed in ice, yet undeniable.

Inside, the cave plunged steeply. Malik followed the path, his headlamp catching glimmers of blue veins streaking through the stone, as if the entire island were laced with floatstone. The deeper he went, the warmer it became. Soon, he was peeling off layers of insulated clothing.

After what felt like hours of descent, the narrow passage opened into a vast cavern – and Malik froze, breath caught in his throat. The chamber was alive with an impossible ecosystem: plants that shouldn't exist at this altitude, animals that gazed at him without fear, and everywhere, a soft blue glow.

At the center of it all, suspended in midair, hovered a perfect sphere of floatstone – larger than anything Malik had ever seen, pulsing with what could only be described as a heartbeat.

At last, the Darkness echoed. *The seedpod. The key to the Plan.*

Malik approached slowly, mesmerized by the pulsing blue light. The sphere was perhaps four feet in diameter, unlike any floatstone he'd worked with throughout his career.

"What is it?" he whispered aloud.

The new life for the world. The nodes of the pattern.

"I don't understand," Malik said, circling the floating sphere.

Understanding isn't necessary. Action is. The seedpod must be freed. The island must descend. The Plan must continue.

Malik hesitated, looking around at the thriving ecosystem. "If I remove this… everything here dies."

Nothing truly dies, the Darkness insisted. *It transforms. Changes. This has happened before. It will happen again. The cycle must complete.*

For a moment, a flicker of doubt passed through Malik's mind. After twenty years of obsession – of following the voice that had consumed his life – he finally stood before his goal… and hesitated.

Do not falter now, the Darkness urged. *You are my instrument. My hands in this world.*

Malik opened his pack and took out the tools he prepared. They were precise instruments meant for harvesting floatstone without causing any fractures. But as he approached the seedpod, he quickly realized they were useless. The sphere resisted every attempt, its surface impervious to all the methods he knew.

"I can't take it from here," he said through clenched teeth.

Not with those. There is another way.

The Darkness led him to a distant section of the chamber where the ceiling thinned. For two days, Malik labored without pause, swinging his pickaxe again and again to weaken the rock above – creating a passage through which the core could rise, if he could break it into fragments.

He slept only in brief, ragged intervals. This time, his dreams dragged him into fire: a burning forest stretching endlessly in all directions. The heat pulsed against his skin in waves, massive trees exploding into columns of flame around him as he ran blindly.

Then the flames would take him completely while the fire wall towered overhead, boring into his eyes, filling his mouth, burning him from the inside out. He'd feel himself turning to ash, disintegrating into nothing while some essential part of him remained conscious, experiencing death twice over. Every time he woke gasping, sheets soaked with sweat, the Darkness was waiting, whispering, *Continue. You are nearly done.*

At last, the ceiling gave way, revealing a glimpse of open sky – like a window.

"Window…" Something shifted inside Malik when he mouthed the word. "Window, just like the one Lisha had wanted."

The simple word pierced through decades of obsession. That humble dream – a room with a window – had seemed so small once. Now it felt more real, more human than the glorious Plan of Darkness.

He was tired of chasing something that wasn't his own desire. Sacrificed everything for goals he'd never chosen. But this – this single memory of Lisha, of their simple hopes together – belonged truly to him.

Reluctantly, he returned to the sphere. The ecosystem was already changing – disturbed by two days of his hacking and slashing. The animals had scattered temporarily into the tunnels, hiding from the noise and activity. The plants had shriveled slightly, feeling the cold air coming from the opening. However, the perfect blue sphere remained, pulsing with that steady, impossible rhythm.

Break it and haul the pieces to the opening.

Malik stood mesmerized, gripping the pickaxe. He had chased it for years, had urged for the mineral, for this immaculate floatstone.

And the thought struck him that destroying this beauty was something beyond his ability.

You need to push the pieces through, the Darkness commanded. *We are almost there.*

Instead, he turned and ran to the opening, climbed into it and reached for the island's edge. The voice in his head shouted commands, but he barely heard it. For the first time in decades, Malik felt a strange clarity. He wasn't serving the Darkness's plan anymore. This was his choice. His action.

Malik stepped to the edge and looked down at the swirling gray mass below. For years, he had thought of this moment and it had haunted him – but now, standing at the brink, he felt something unexpected: peace.

Come back, the Plan needs you. You must destroy the sphere.

Malik Dunn – once a simple miner from the Kingdom of Azurath, former member of Parliament and the Miners' Guild Senior Member – understood that the nightmare that had haunted him from the beginning was becoming real. And he took a step into the void.

ALEX O.HARB

READER

OF THE

WIND

READER OF THE WIND

An eagle shrieked, and Kora ducked for cover, pulling Harrik down with her behind a rocky outcrop. Her heart pounded against her ribs. Beneath her fingers on his wrist, she felt his pulse – fast and fearful, mirroring her own.

"She saw us at the nest," Kora whispered, her breath blooming white in the thin, cold air of the Heights. "I told you we shouldn't have come so close."

Harrik's eyes – deep brown, the brown of dried feathers – were wide with a thrilling mix of fear and excitement. At twelve, he was already bold to the point of recklessness: endlessly curious, never one to back down from a dare.

"It's okay," he whispered back – though his racing pulse betrayed him. "She won't spot us here."

The angry mother eagle circled, her huge wings casting a fleeting shadow over them. Fifteen feet, easily, tip to tip.

"Just one more look," Harrik begged. "I've never seen eggs this early in the season."

Kora bit her lip. She was thirteen, the older one, already learning how the air currents shaped everything up here. She should have known better. Yet here she was – hiding from an angry bird after sneaking too close to its nest.

"Okay, on three," she gave in. "Quick peek – then we run."

Harrik grinned, and Kora felt a flutter in her chest – one that had nothing to do with the eagle overhead.

"One… two… *three*!"

They bolted from cover, scrambling to the edge of the nesting plateau. The eagle dove instantly, screeching – talons out, ready to defend her blue-speckled eggs.

"Run!" Kora shouted, grabbing Harrik's hand.

They raced away, leaping over rocks, sliding on ice patches, laughing breathlessly despite the danger closing in. The wind whistled past Kora's ears, carrying the powerful *whoosh* of wings right behind them. They reached the safety of the downward path just as the eagle, unwilling to leave her eggs unguarded for long, pulled up.

Out of range, they collapsed onto the ground, gasping, laughter catching in their throats.

"Did you see?" Harrik asked when he could talk. "Three eggs! The elders say that's a blessing for the tribe."

Kora nodded, still smiling. "Your father will say it's a good sign." She didn't say what they both knew: as the chief's son, good signs tended to point Harrik's way.

"I'll tell him you saw them first," Harrik said, bumping her shoulder with his. "Your eyes are better."

"And you run faster," she said, bumping him back. "Good team."

They sat on the sun-warmed rock, legs dangling over the immense drop, looking out at the endless sky scattered with floating islets. Below them lay Roost, spread across its terraces – the most permanent home their people had known. Smoke drifted up from cooking fires, and eagles soared between platforms, carrying people about their day.

"Race you to the channel?" Harrik asked, already on his feet.

"You wish," Kora retorted, scrambling up – though she knew he'd probably win.

As they ran down the path toward the channel that supplied Roost's water, Kora found herself watching Harrik – the way the sun caught his dark hair, the sound of his laugh, the sure way he moved.

That was the first day she realized her feelings for the chief's son were changing. He wasn't just her friend anymore. It was something more complicated, scarier, and more exciting than outrunning any eagle.

———

Six years passed.

Kora stood with the tribe, her fingers tracing the swirling wind-pattern tattoos on her forearms – marks showing she was learning the wind-reader's craft. The tattoos weren't just decoration; they mapped the invisible language of the air.

But she wasn't looking at her arms. Her eyes were fixed on Harrik. He was eighteen now, walking toward the Eagle Cliff for his bonding ceremony. He looked impressive in his ceremonial feather cloak, ritual patterns painted across his bare chest, his face shimmering faintly with blue heartstone dust.

"He was always marked for great things," her mother murmured beside her. Kora glanced over; her mother's own tattoos were faded now. "But don't forget what I told you, daughter."

Kora swallowed. They'd had this talk before. Her friendship with Harrik had quietly deepened into something else – secret meetings, a hesitant first kiss, whispered hopes.

"They will never let him marry you," her mother said quietly, for Kora's ears only. "He's the chief's son, raised to be the best. You aren't seen as a suitable match for him, Kora."

"Is there anything wrong that we love each other?" Kora whispered back, aware of the people nearby.

Her mother sighed softly. "Love isn't wrong, dear. But politics seldom cares for love."

Before Kora could answer, the drums began. Chief Berrik, Harrik's father, stepped forward holding the ceremonial eagle-call whistle, carved from bone and inlaid with heartstone. The crowd hushed as he handed it to his son.

Harrik took it solemnly, but as he turned to the cliff edge, his eyes found Kora's. Just a look, a tiny nod, a flicker of a smile – but it felt like a promise. Whatever politics demanded, what they shared was real.

The drums grew louder as Harrik stepped to the very edge. He raised the whistle and blew a sharp, complex call into the thin air.

Then he spread his arms and jumped.

Kora's breath caught. Her stomach plunged as he vanished. She knew the ritual, knew most survived – but fear seized her. One in twenty didn't make it back.

Time stretched. The tribe held its breath.

Then a huge brown eagle soared into view, Harrik clinging to its back. It circled three times, Harrik raising his arms in triumph.

The crowd cheered wildly. Kora shouted too, relief washing over her, pushing aside her mother's warnings. Harrik had passed his final trial. He was now considered a man – ready for council, ready for hunts, ready for marriage.

The eagle landed, and Chief Berrik proudly embraced his son. Harrik accepted the elders' congratulations gracefully, but his eyes kept finding Kora.

Later, when the feast was winding down, they found a moment alone.

"I heard your voice in the wind," Harrik whispered, his face still bright with success. "When I jumped. It helped."

Kora smiled, though the warnings lingered. "You were never short on courage."

"It's easier to be brave," he replied, his hand briefly brushing hers before they had to separate, "when you have something worth coming back to."

Watching him rejoin his father, surrounded by important families, Kora felt a familiar worry. How long could stolen moments last against duty and expectation? She was just a wind-reader's daughter, not a strategic match for a future chief.

But tonight, she let herself hope.

———

Kora sat at the edge of Whisper Islet, eyes closed, feeling the invisible currents flow past. At twenty-three, she was becoming known as a skilled wind-reader, sensing shifts others couldn't.

She'd spent the last month practicing alone on this small, high islet, where the winds were cleaner, sharper. It was lonely, but she needed the focus.

And the solitude gave her space to think about Harrik. About their hidden relationship, balanced precariously for five years since his bonding. Five years of secret meetings, watching him take on more duties while she honed her skills. Five years of him politely turning down the marriage prospects his parents presented.

It couldn't go on forever.

The wind shifted, carrying a faint, familiar scent – pine and heartstone. Kora opened her eyes. Only Harrik would come here.

"Took you long enough," she said without turning.

He chuckled. "You knew I was coming."

"The wind told me," she confirmed, looking over her shoulder.

He looked more like the leader now – leaner, more sure of himself. But his deep brown eyes were the same – warm, kind, with that spark of mischief only she seemed to ignite.

"I missed you," he said, sitting beside her.

Kora leaned against him, just for a moment. "I missed you too."

They sat quietly, watching the sunset paint the floating islets gold and purple. Below, the magnificent clouds glowed softly.

"Come back to Roost," Harrik said finally. "Finish your training there."

Kora shook her head. "I need this time – to think. To figure out what I really want."

"And what's that?" he asked carefully.

She turned to him. "Do you ever wonder what's below the clouds? Or past the high streams?"

Harrik frowned. "Kingdoms. Traders. You know that."

"But farther down? We know of Depths – that great storm beneath the kingdoms. Legends say there's nothing below it. But no one really knows."

"Old stories," he dismissed. "Why ask now?"

Kora took a breath. "In Caligan, in the Technocracy, there's a university. They study winds with science, instruments, math. Meteorology, they call it."

His frown deepened. "You've been talking to lowlander traders."

"Yes. And their way of understanding weather… it fits with our ways. Together, the two could–"

"You're thinking of going down there," Harrik interrupted, sounding shocked. "To study?"

Kora met his eyes. "I'm thinking about it."

"But you belong here. With the tribe. With–" He stopped.

"With you?" she finished softly. "Do I, Harrik? Do I really belong here?"

The pain in his eyes answered before he spoke. "My responsibilities – Father expects me to lead. The tribe comes first."

She nodded slowly. "And a chief needs a suitable wife," she said, bitterness creeping in. "Not just a wind-reader."

"That's not fair," he protested. "I've refused everyone else."

"For how long? Five more years? Ten? Sneaking around until we're old?"

He looked away, jaw clenched. "You know what's expected of me."

She held his gaze. "Then give me a real reason to stay."

He reached for her hand but stopped just short. "I don't want to lose you."

Kora's voice barely rose above a whisper. "I hate losing you too."

Then she leaned against him – gentle, lingering. And though neither said more, the air between them softened.

Later, lying together on the grass and looking at the night sky, he spoke of his dreams.

"Someday, I'll have a real beard," he murmured against her shoulder, rubbing his chin with a wry smile. "Seven braids, for the seven peaks. I'll make Roost the strongest settlement in the Heights."

Kora smiled faintly.

After a pause, she spoke too. She told him about the heartstone goggles she'd heard of – lenses that supposedly let you see the wind currents.

"Only the best wind-readers of the past were rumored to have them," she said. "I'll have them someday."

"I'm sure you will," he chuckled. "At least your dream requires skill. The beard just grows by itself."

They laughed beneath the stars, sharing dreams like they could hold off the future. For a while, it almost felt true.

But dawn approached, cold and uncompromising.

The sky was pale with morning when Kora finally spoke again, her voice barely above the hush of wind in the grass.

"I'm leaving for Caligan in three days," she said quietly as they dressed. "I booked passage."

Harrik froze. "Three days? That soon?"

"I decided months ago," she said, fastening her cloak. "I just needed to be sure."

He nodded slowly, his expression unreadable.

"And now you are." His voice was flat. Resigned.

"I can't stay stuck, Harrik. I have to move forward."

"Without me," he said.

She paused as she strapped on her pack. "That's your choice," she replied, keeping her voice even. "You know where I'll be."

As he prepared to leave on his eagle, they faced each other one last time on the wind-swept platform.

"If you asked me to stay," Kora said, giving him one final chance, "not in secret – not someday – but truly, with a life we don't have to hide... I would."

His face was tight with pain. He looked at her for a long moment. "Kora... I just can't."

Her throat tightened, but she nodded. She'd known. Still, it hurt. "Then I wish you well, future Chief."

He reached for her, but she stepped back. A clean break – anything less, and she'd never leave.

"May the winds guide you," Harrik said, falling back on tradition.

"And bring you wisdom," she replied, the words dry in her mouth.

She didn't watch him fly away. She didn't trust herself.

Instead, she turned to the wind, letting the currents thread around her fingers, pulling her forward – toward the unknown, toward herself, and a purpose that didn't need permission.

———

"You don't look like a Technocrat," Professor Valen had said during her first week, examining her tribal wind-reader tattoos with undisguised skepticism. "Our methods are precise. Scientific. Not... folklore and feeling."

Six months later, when she challenged his equations on vertical air currents, using data she'd gathered from her own observations, he'd dismissed her in front of the entire lecture hall.

"Perhaps in the Heights, this passes for methodology," he'd said coolly. "Here, we require actual evidence, not mystical intuition."

Her tribal training had taught her to mask her emotions, but now her mask slipped. The humiliation and rage had shown plainly on her face.

"The winds don't care about your degrees, Professor," she'd replied, her voice too loud in the suddenly silent hall. "They move as they will, whether or not your equations can capture them."

That outburst had nearly cost her place at the university. It taught her the first of many hard lessons about being an outsider in the Technocracy's world: brilliance alone wasn't enough. She would have to become fluent in two languages of knowledge – the tribal wisdom of her people and the scientific precision of her professors.

———

The Caligan market was a loud, bustling mess of noise and smells – people yelling in Trade Speech, machines clanking, steam hissing. Two years into her university studies, Kora still found the chaos overwhelming after the high, quiet airs of home.

She wore her practical student clothes – trousers, a jacket with pockets, sleeves hiding most of her wind-reader tattoos. She probably looked like any other Caligan student, except for the way she sometimes tilted her head, unconsciously feeling the air currents, a habit she couldn't break.

"Imports from the Heights!" a vendor shouted. "Real tribal goods! Eagle feathers! Heartstone charms!"

Kora stopped. Homesickness hit her sharply. Most "Heights artifacts" sold down here were cheap fakes, but she drifted towards the stall anyway.

Amidst the junk – clumsy carvings, dyed feathers, cloudy rocks labeled *heartstone* – one piece stood out. A small warrior figure, carved from bone. He held an axe, his face stern. And his beard… Kora caught her breath. It was long, full, and carved into seven distinct braids.

Harrik's dream.

"Interested in the warrior, miss?" the vendor asked. "Real bone carving. Old piece."

Kora picked it up. It felt cool, solid. The carving was good, much better than the rest; maybe it was authentic. It wasn't Harrik, but it *felt* like him – the stance, the carved responsibility in the face, and that seven-braided beard. It hit her hard.

"How much?" she asked quietly.

The price was outrageous, almost all the money she had. But she paid it. This little piece of bone felt like an anchor, something real connecting her to the life, the love, she'd left behind.

Clutching the statuette, Kora walked away from the noisy market. Her studies were going well, her mind busy with wind physics and meteorology, but part of her was still back in the Heights, with Roost, with Harrik. She'd chosen this path, but it came with a constant, dull ache of loneliness. The statuette wouldn't fix that, but holding it felt like holding onto something vital.

———

By her third year, even Valen had been forced to acknowledge her work. By her fourth, she was charting wind patterns no Technocrat had ever properly documented.

Kora, twenty-seven, had finished her studies and was making a name for herself as a weather expert, consulting for airship routes.

News from home came rarely. Roost was stable, tribal life back home was quiet.

Then the message arrived: Chief Berrik had died in an accident. Harrik would be formally named the new Chief of the Windclaw.

Duty – and a stubborn ache in her heart – pulled her back.

The trip felt strange. She traveled as a respected professional from the Technocracy, not just a tribal member returning home. Roost felt the same, yet different. The air – sharper. The sounds – eagle calls, High Tongue, funeral drums – unfamiliar yet deeply known.

She saw Harrik by the ceremonial fire. He wore the chief's full regalia now, his father's cloak on his shoulders. His beard was longer, styled in the seven braids he'd once dreamed of. He looked older, heavier – the burden of leadership had settled on him.

Then Kora saw the woman standing slightly behind him, her hand on his arm. Pregnant. Harrik's wife.

It hit Kora like a physical blow. The blood drained from her face. Of course. Life went on. He'd done his duty, made a good match, started his family. Their young dream was over, truly over.

She couldn't stay. Clutching the bone warrior in her pocket – her companion for these past four years – she turned to leave, hoping to slip away unnoticed.

"Kora?"

Harrik's voice. She stopped and turned slowly.

He came toward her, his expression hard to read. "I didn't know if you'd come."

"I came to honor your father," she said stiffly, professionally. "He was a great chief."

"Yes," Harrik agreed. He indicated the woman. "Kora, this is Tyra – my wife."

Tyra nodded politely, her eyes curious. Kora gave a small nod in return, murmuring a greeting in High Tongue.

The silence felt heavy. Kora could feel eyes on her.

"I should return to Caligan," Kora said quickly. "Work…"

Harrik nodded, his eyes lingering on her face. "Thank you for coming, Kora. It means… a lot."

She escaped onto the waiting transport, her composure cracking only once she was alone. The trip back down was a blur. The past was sealed. Her future was in the winds, in her work, in the solitary life she was building.

Time flew. Over the years, Kora became a leading figure in meteorology. Now in her forties, Kora Skyheart was sought after across Azoria. Her unique mix of tribal instinct and scientific training gave her unmatched insight into the world's complex weather.

She charted dangerous winds, documented the Maelstrom south of the Drift Lords, developed ways to predict seasonal shifts, and published papers blending the tribal ways with science. She advised leaders, gave lectures, and occasionally dealt with arrogant men who thought her skills were for sale.

Her life was busy, challenging, successful, and profoundly lonely.

She hardly ever went back to Roost. Years ago, at a naming ceremony, she had seen Harrik's son – around twelve then, looking exactly like Harrik at that age. The resemblance hurt, confirming her choice to stay away. She heard news sometimes: Harrik was a strong, respected chief, uniting tribes. Tyra had given him a daughter too. Around that same time, she learned her brother, Arvid, had a son as well – Toryn, her first and only nephew.

Kora had never thought seriously about having children herself, or starting a family. The occasional men in her life were neither stable nor husband material.

One evening, Kora was alone in her clean but bland quarters at a Technocracy outpost. She had just routed a zeppelin caravan through a fierce ice storm and politely rejected yet another awkward advance from a wealthy merchant. She held the bone warrior statuette, worn smooth from years of unconscious touch.

She had achieved her professional goals: independent, respected, accomplished. But the things that anchored others – family, love, home – were missing. She was admired, but not truly connected. Belonging everywhere meant belonging nowhere.

The old loneliness surfaced, sharp and insistent. Maybe it was time, she thought, to find somewhere closer to her roots. Not Roost – that door felt firmly closed – but perhaps another Heights tribe. Somewhere, her skills could serve a community. Somewhere, the air felt like home.

Kora found a measure of peace working with the Cloudrunner Tribe, whose islets floated astonishingly high.

For two years, she served as their wind-reader, charting unpredictable currents and teaching what she could of weather modeling. The Cloudrunners respected her – admired her insight, trusted her guidance – but she was never quite one of them.

They listened, but they did not confide. They praised, but did not embrace. When a seat opened on the Elder Council, it was quietly given to a native-born tracker with far less experience. Kora said nothing, but the message was clear: she was useful, but not truly theirs.

Not Windclaw. Not Cloudrunner. A guest. A ghost. Still adrift.

Then a Windclaw eagle rider arrived, exhausted, bearing news. Her younger brother, Arvid, and his wife, Elvira, had been scouting Ember Islet when it fell into the Depths below. They didn't escaped the fall.

Their son – her nephew – Toryn, fourteen, was orphaned.

Something shifted inside Kora – sudden and fierce, like a wind changing direction. Her careful life, her detachment, her solitude – fell away. Duty, sharp and clear, took its place. Toryn. Her blood. Her last link to the Skyheart name. He needed her.

The path that had led away from Roost more than two decades ago now led back. Back home.

The memorial for Arvid and Elvira was somber, the familiar tribal chants echoing Kora's private grief. There were no bodies – only names and memories carried by the wind.

She stood at Toryn's side. No words passed between them during the ceremony – none were needed. She had already taken him in, already moved back into the family house where she and Arvid had once grown up.

He was tall and thin, trying hard to look strong. But he only looked lost. Kora remembered the moment, a day earlier, when she'd told him gently, "I'll be your guardian now. Your father was a good man." He had nodded, swallowed, and said only, "He taught me… things."

Now he faced becoming a man without either parent. But not alone.

That evening, Kora stood at the islet's edge – the same rocky outcrop where she and Harrik had once hidden from an angry eagle. The wind curled around her like an old friend.

"I thought I might find you here."

She turned. Harrik stood silhouetted against the fading light, older now, the lines at his eyes deeper. Silver streaked the seven braids of his beard. He wore his authority lightly – the powerful chief who had united tribes and made Windclaw the strongest clan in memory. Ritual scars traced his arms.

"Chief Harrik," she said with a nod.

He heard it – and his reply came gently. "I am, and always was, just Harrik to you, Kora." He sat beside her.

"Tyra died three winters ago," he said quietly, answering the question she hadn't voiced. "Fever."

Kora sighed, hearing the ache in his voice. "I'm so sorry, Harrik."

A pause. "Kids have left already?"

"Son left for the Technocracy two years back – wants to study engineering." A wry smile touched his mouth. "Parents ruined my life by expecting me to become someone. I won't do the same to him." He paused, still smiling. "Daughter married a Stormrunner and moved. She seems happy."

He turned to her. "It's just me now. And Roost."

"And me," Kora said softly. "And Toryn. I'm staying – to raise him." *That, and only that. No other reason,* she thought, her discipline hiding her confusion at being near Harrik again.

They sat in silence, decades of unspoken words and separate lives hanging between them.

Then Harrik reached into a pouch. "I kept something," he said, unwrapping a small leather parcel. Inside lay goggles – lenses of clear, flawless heartstone. The kind she'd dreamed of, twenty-four years ago.

"Harrik…" she breathed, stunned. "These goggles… you found them?"

"Bought them from a trader. After you left," he said. "Always hoped… maybe you'd come back."

Tears pricked her eyes. Kora reached into her pocket and drew out the small bone warrior. "And I," she whispered, "kept this."

Harrik took the figure, his thumb tracing the worn lines, the seven carved braids. Understanding flowed between them – two lives lived apart, bound by memories and the tokens they had carried close all these years.

He looked up, his deep eyes meeting hers. The Chief's reserve slipped away, and for a moment, he was only the man she had known – the one she'd once loved and lost.

Slowly, he reached out and touched her cheek. Kora leaned into the warmth of his hand, eyes closing. After so many years adrift on separate winds, they had found the same shore again.

He bent and kissed her. It wasn't the fire of youth, but something quieter, steadier – a kiss of regret, resilience, and the quiet promise of a second chance.

When they pulled apart, they sat close, her head resting against his shoulder. Two weathered souls beneath a familiar sky. The wind curled around them, rich with the scent of pine, heartstone, and home. The future was uncertain, but for the first time in decades, Kora felt at home.

ALEX O. HARB

RATIONAL ELEMENT

RATIONAL ELEMENT

Return to Your Roots

Theon Reeves was good at his work. Really good. He was the top marketing guy on Taurus. His office wall was covered with awards and thank-you letters from campaigns that had changed entire industries. He had already made millions when he wasn't even twenty-seven.

The only problem was that each success felt more and more empty. Every campaign convincing people to want things they didn't need felt like manipulation.

What he really wanted was simple: retire, buy a nice house, find a hobby, raise kids with Helena, and live a life without fake desires and manufactured urgency. And now, his millions meant nothing in the current real estate market.

The worry began as a knot in his stomach the moment he saw the house prices. Theon stared at the numbers on his tablet, doing the same math that had become a daily torment. The prices were insane – hundreds of times what his parents had paid for their home just a generation earlier. Even after years of successful campaigns and careful saving, he couldn't afford anything decent.

Sure, they could still buy an apartment. Maybe even a miniature townhouse. Or a plot of land – out in the frozen tundra.

"Still looking?" Helena asked, leaning over his shoulder. Her blonde hair was tied in a simple braid that fell forward as she studied the screen. In her last months of pregnancy, she moved carefully, one hand resting on her belly.

"The prices keep going up," he said, scrolling through pictures of homes that might as well have been on distant planets. "People from the Orion Arm keep moving in, and there aren't enough homes. It's like watching an auction where everyone has more money than sense."

Helena squeezed his shoulder with her free hand. "We could look at something smaller. Maybe farther from the city."

Theon shook his head, feeling frustrated. "You wanted a garden – I promised you that. And space for our family." He put the tablet down and rubbed his temples, feeling the weight of success that couldn't buy happiness. "We saved for years, followed every financial rule, and we're worse off now than when we started."

"We could try one of the new colonies," Helena suggested, though her voice carried doubt. "I hear Proxima Ceta needs plant scientists."

He sighed. "Proxima Ceta is a mining operation with poisonous air," Theon replied. He had researched every option until he was sick of it. "New Taurus is controlled by that religious group that requires genetic testing. Horizon has acidic rains that eat through buildings in five years. The others are either too expensive, too dangerous, or don't accept new people."

Helena settled beside him at their tiny kitchen table, moving carefully. "So what will we do?"

"What if we don't go to an existing colony at all?" he said slowly. "What if we try something completely new?"

That night, after Helena went to bed and he could hear her steady breathing, Theon began the search that would change everything. The excitement built slowly as he dug through survey files, his mind already spinning with possibilities.

Then he found Azoria, buried in decades-old Federation survey data. It was marked «*Unique Anomaly – Low Priority*» and shelved when more profitable projects came along. An automated drone had found the planet and conducted a preliminary survey. Landmasses floated in perfectly breathable air, waiting to be explored. The survey notes called them «*stable megastructures of unknown, possibly artificial origin*». The islands' anti-gravity properties were flagged with a red exclamation mark and a note: «*Further research required!*»

Theon traced the cluster of floating islands on the map – just a small constellation near the equator, covering only a few percent of the planet. But the weather there was mild, almost tropical, as if inviting humans in.

Yet the severe electromagnetic interference had scared off the corporate developers. Several research probes were launched, but none reached the surface. Perpetual storms covered the entire planet below. The survey AI didn't attribute them to meteorological causes but hypothesized a low-level energy field encircling the globe. It hovered at about 3,000 feet, causing severe weather disturbance, depleting batteries and draining power even from the wires. After several attempts and a brief ecosystem analysis, the survey craft gave the planet a low priority, cleared it for human visitation, and left.

To Theon, that meant something beautiful: a world where people would have to rely on themselves – and each other. Floating islands. A mild climate. Plants and animals were already there, likely seeded during pre-Federation terraforming. No people, no governments, no corporations. No endless noise of modern civilization.

As he read, the excitement grew into something almost joyful. This wasn't just a solution to their housing problem – this was the answer to everything wrong with their current world.

There was no way two people with a newborn could survive there alone, so his instincts kicked in: if there was no town to live in, they would need to move in with a town. By dawn, he had written the foundation of what would become the most successful – and most devastating – marketing campaign of his career.

"Return to Your Roots! Live like your ancestors did," he typed, his fingers moving with the certainty of inspiration. "Work with your hands, build your own home, grow your own food. Forget robots, AI, endless news feeds, and manufactured desires. Return to authentic human life."

The Campaign Takes Flight

"You want us to move to an uncolonized planet?" Helena asked over breakfast as she scrolled through his early proposal. "With the baby coming?"

"Not just us," Theon said, the words tumbling out with barely contained excitement. "We would recruit people – skilled people who think alike. Farmers, doctors, engineers, carpenters – specialists who can build a real community from the ground up."

"But not just any specialists," Theon clarified, anticipating her next question. "We would select people who understand that technology will be useless. We'll need engineers who can work from blueprints, farmers who can measure soil acidity with chemical kits, and carpenters who can use an axe. We'd spend the entire journey training, printing manuals, preparing for life without electricity. Every colonist would arrive with tools and printed books relevant to their field."

Helena's eyebrows rose as she read. "This sounds like a marketing campaign."

"Because it is," he admitted, grinning. "The best one I've ever thought of. We're not just selling a product – we're offering a completely different life. Freedom from the complexity that's choking us."

"And how exactly would you convince skilled professionals to abandon civilization and follow us to… what did you call it? A floating rock?"

Theon's excitement bubbled over as he leaned forward. "By telling them the truth – that we're offering what everyone secretly wants. Look at the stress rates, the depression numbers, the surveys about job satisfaction. People are miserable, Helena. They're drowning in bureaucracy and complexity, working at jobs they hate to buy things they don't need."

He pulled up population studies on his tablet, the marketing analyst in him coming alive. "Skilled professionals feel trapped. They have expertise but no control. They earn good money but can't afford the life they want. They're burned out on technology but dependent on it."

"So you'd market… what? Authenticity?"

"Exactly." The vision became clear as he spoke. "Return to the basics that made humanity thrive for thousands of years. Real community where everyone knows their neighbors. Work that has visible, meaningful results. A place where your children can grow up without screens. Where families eat dinner together. Where people solve problems by talking to each other instead of filing complaints."

Helena set down the tablet, studying his face. "You're serious about this."

"I've never been more serious about anything." He reached across the table and took her hand. "Think about it – you could have not just a garden, but acres. You could use all your plant knowledge in a place that's never seen a proper botanist. Our child could grow up in fresh air, learning real skills, being part of something real."

She was quiet for a long moment, and he could see her working through the implications. Finally, she smiled – the first genuinely excited expression he had seen from her in weeks.

"You know I've always loved the old Norse sagas," she said thoughtfully. "Stories of brave people exploring unknown lands, building communities." She squeezed his hand. "Tell me more about these floating islands."

As he talked, Helena reached for her sketchpad and began drawing a simple picture – a floating island with a single tree on top and a waterfall cascading down from it. Theon felt the future taking shape.

Neither of them realized that the marketing campaign they were planning would attract not dozens, but thousands of people seeking escape from the modern world.

Going Viral

Six months later, Theon stood in his temporary office, surrounded by application forms that covered every surface. What began as a plan to recruit about eighty skilled colonists had turned into something extraordinary.

"We have over four thousand applications," announced Maria Santos, the project coordinator he had hired when the workload became overwhelming. "And more are arriving daily."

Theon stared at the numbers, excited and terrified at the same time. The *Return to Your Roots* campaign had resonated so powerfully that applications poured in from across the Federation.

"How many can we actually transport?" he asked.

"The first ship can carry a maximum of five hundred people," Maria replied. "But we have applications from nearly twenty families per day. At this rate, we'll need many ships over several years just to send everyone who has expressed interest."

Helena, now nursing baby Erik while reviewing plant supply lists, looked up with concern. "That's not what we planned, Theon. Eighty people is a community. Thousands is…"

"A civilization," he finished quietly, the weight of realization settling on his shoulders.

But the applications kept coming. Engineers, farmers, teachers, craftspeople. Families who wanted their children to grow up outside of concrete jungles.

Each application told the same story: successful people trapped in systems they couldn't change, seeking an authentic life.

"We could limit the first wave to the original eighty," Helena suggested. "Turn away the rest."

Theon looked at Erik, sleeping peacefully in Helena's arms. He thought of the people who were ready to trust his vision enough to abandon their old lives.

"No," he decided. "We'll find a way to make it work. These people are counting on us."

The weight of five hundred lives pressed down on his shoulders like a physical burden.

Five Hundred Souls

A year later, Theon stood on the bridge of the Pioneer, watching Azoria grow larger on the main screen. He thought he would feel at ease, finally bringing this to completion. But something told him it wasn't time to relax – it was only the beginning.

They had five hundred people aboard this ship alone. The vessel was overcrowded, supplies stretched thin, but the enthusiasm was infectious.

Beside him stood Helena with Erik in her arms. The boy was cheerfully babbling and smiling at the bridge staff. He was just over a year old now, having spent his first birthday aboard the Pioneer. Every time Theon looked at that tiny, peaceful face, he felt the full weight of what he had set in motion.

"Final approach checks complete," announced Miguel Reyes, a young man who was their navigator and a former Flight Academy graduate. Miguel had been one of the first to respond to the campaign – a man exhausted by military bureaucracy and questioning his life choices.

"Thank you, Miguel," Theon replied, though his attention was fixed on the view ahead. "Take us down."

"I can't believe we're doing this," Helena murmured, her voice filled with wonder as she studied the floating islands on the close-up screen. "Look at that – it's exactly like the drawing I made!"

Theon glanced at the simple sketch she'd drawn during her pregnancy, now framed and mounted near the navigation station. It had hung on their refrigerator on Taurus, replacing the usual tasks and appointments that had now become so irrelevant and distant.

His campaign had worked too well. Before they left, he had met with Maria to finalize the handover. He had formed the "Azoria Colonization Project" as a legal entity and transferred all rights and control to her. It was now a business.

"The demand is incredible," Maria had said, showing him projections on her tablet. "This isn't just a colony, Theon – it's a brand. The *Return to Your Roots* message can be licensed. We can sell passage, supplies, training modules… this is a money machine."

Theon had felt a pang of unease at her words, but he pushed it aside. "Just make sure they're good people, Maria. And that the supplies are what they'll actually need."

"Don't worry, boss," she had promised with a sharp, commercial smile. "I'll keep a steady stream of colonists – and revenue – coming your way. *Return to Your Roots* will work for a decade at least. Don't forget to send me nice photos of you relaxing!"

He had smiled then, knowing that there would be no photos. Maria was a good person, but she only cared about success, without digging deep into the details of what they were selling.

"Maria, I need you to understand – we won't have any connection with you. And we're not leaving the planet. Ever. I don't need the revenue – just keep sending supplies with each ship."

She hesitated. "But how will we know the colony is still functioning? That you're all still alive?"

"Every approaching ship will scan the islands from orbit, check for signs of settlements and activity, and decide if it's safe to land. Before they touch down, they'll relay a message back to you."

"Proximity alert," Miguel called out, pulling him from the memory."The electromagnetic field is stronger than the survey data suggested. It's actively draining our power cells. Radio transmission and navigation are already failing."

Theon nodded grimly. This was expected, but experiencing it was different from theoretical knowledge. Warning lights flickered across the control panels as systems began to shut down.

"How severe?" Helena asked, Erik stirring in her arms at the sound of the alarms.

"Worse than projected," Miguel admitted. "We'll have enough power to land and open all the doors before we're completely drained."

The ship shook as they entered the final approach, and everyone buckled up. Through the viewport, Theon could see their destination: a beautiful island with forests, clearings, and a lake near the center. It looked exactly like the paradise he had promised.

The final descent sequence took mere minutes and was a bit rough. "Landing complete," Miguel announced as the Pioneer settled onto solid ground. "Welcome to Azoria."

A cheer went up from the bridge crew and echoed through the ship's communication system. Helena's eyes were bright with tears of joy and wonder. Erik was smiling, looking around at the cheering people with the curiosity that always made Theon's heart ache with love.

They had made it. Against all odds, his vision had become a reality.

Rational Element

"The irrigation system is working perfectly," Helena said as they walked through their first garden. Erik toddled between them, fascinated by everything, his chubby hands reaching for flowers and insects with equal enthusiasm.

Theon nodded, making notes in the leather-bound ledger that had replaced his electronic tablet.

"The crops are exceeding all projections," Helena continued, her excitement evident. "There's something special about this soil – it's as if it was designed for our plants. Perfect acidity, perfect moisture level. And the native grass is good for our livestock."

Helena led the colony's agricultural team, and they had come prepared. Their farming was already sustaining more people and animals than expected. Mild seasons meant they were already harvesting their first crops. That required a lot of manual work: digging, planting, fertilizing, and weeding. But they had an abundance of workers.

"Best news I've heard all week," Theon replied, though his tone carried more weight than relief. The agricultural success was crucial because the supplies wouldn't last forever. Moreover, four more ships had arrived this year as scheduled, carrying nearly fifteen hundred more people, with two additional vessels en route.

The settlement on Liberty Drift now housed nearly two thousand people. Most of them were living in ship hulls and hastily built temporary barracks. The first wave of log cabins was almost ready – all without electricity or running water – while more permanent houses would be delayed for years to come.

"Daddy!" Erik said clearly, one of his first words, and held up a blue flower he had picked.

The simple joy on his son's face cut through Theon's growing worry. This was what mattered – Helena's happiness, Erik's wonder at the world, the chance to build something real together. But the weight of responsibility for so many others made those moments feel increasingly precious and fragile.

"Theon!" a voice called. Garrett Lawson jogged toward them, his hands stained with the blue dust that seemed to get into all his clothes lately. Despite the failing technology, Garrett had adapted quickly, using mechanical tools and basic chemistry for his geological surveys.

"I've found something incredible," Garrett said, slightly breathless from excitement. He held out what looked like a chunk of blue crystal, glowing softly in the afternoon light.

"More mineral samples?" Helena asked, lifting Erik when he reached for her.

"It's not a mineral," Garrett explained, his engineer's enthusiasm obvious. "It's a crystalline lattice… almost like a circuit. It's woven through the island's entire substructure. It doesn't defy gravity; it seems to be actively nullifying it on a quantum level. This isn't geology – it's some kind of… planetary-scale engineering."

Theon studied the crystal, feeling a strange tingling where it touched his skin. "You're certain?"

"As certain as I can be without proper equipment," Garrett replied. "I've run every test I can devise. This material consistently demonstrates anti-gravitational properties and has some kind of charge. It doesn't just push against gravity – it makes the entire object it's attached to lighter."

"And why isn't it floating right now?" Helena asked skeptically.

"Because this specimen was mined from below the current ground level. It's bound to its natural height and won't go farther. But you can't throw it off the island – it will just float nearby. The purer the mineral, the higher it will go and the more it will lift the island or anything else! Purity determines altitude, quantity determines force," Garrett explained. "That's why islands at higher altitudes – we call them the Heights – are so small. They float far above, but with just a whisper of it."

The implications hit Theon immediately. This discovery could revolutionize transportation, construction, everything about how they lived.

"It needs a proper scientific designation," Helena noted practically.

Garrett chuckled, some of his humor showing through the scientific excitement. "Well, considering how it defies conventional physics, I thought we might call it the Rational Element. A bit of irony, since it behaves completely irrationally by normal standards. Between us, it's just floatstone."

Theon smiled at his friend's wit. "Rational Element it is. But Garrett, this information stays between us for now. We need to understand the implications before word spreads. We don't want people extracting too much and having the whole island collapse."

"Agreed," Garrett said, carefully wrapping the sample. "But Theon, this changes everything. Not just for us, but potentially for the entire Federation if we ever reestablish contact."

Walking back toward the settlement with Helena and Erik, Theon paused at the hill overlooking their growing community. Below them, hundreds of people worked on various projects – building, tending gardens, crafting. Children played in safe areas while adults collaborated on solutions to daily challenges.

The key to their success wasn't just the fertile soil, but their economic model. They had established a communal system where everyone worked according to their abilities. Helena's team managed large-scale food production, while others focused on construction, tool-making, and child care. Resources were managed through community councils that tracked needs and allocated labor efficiently.

It was beautiful. It was everything he had promised in his campaign. And somehow, it was actually working.

The Weight of Success

Two years later, the colony council meeting had grown far beyond the intimate discussions Theon had originally envisioned. The large meeting hall, organized in the Pioneers' dining room, buzzed with conversations.

"On the population update," Miguel said. His skills made him essential as the settlement administrator. "We now have approximately thirty-five hundred residents across the main settlement and five satellite communities. We have a steady stream of new arrivals and natural births."

Theon nodded, though the number sent a familiar chill through him. His marketing campaign continued to attract new arrivals monthly. People continued to respond to his *Return to Your Roots* message, often arriving with unrealistic expectations about the ease of "primitive" life.

"Resource allocation is becoming critical," reported Selena Vale, chief medical officer and one of the original crew. "Medical supplies are adequate for now, but if growth continues at this rate…"

"It will continue," Theon said grimly. "I've received word that two more ships are being prepared. Eight hundred more people combined."

A murmur of concern spread through the council. They had developed sustainable resource cycles to manage growth. Agricultural innovations and careful livestock management could support the population. The real challenge was organizing labor and distribution systems.

Leopold Arkwright, who had become their chief librarian and keeper of knowledge, cleared his throat. "The Library expansion is keeping pace with population growth," he reported. "We now have three dedicated buildings housing our original book collection and detailed records of everything we've learned about Azoria. The preservation work is crucial – we're documenting discoveries and techniques that could be vital for future generations."

Theon felt a surge of gratitude toward Leopold. The Library had become more than a repository of knowledge; it was evolving into the institutional memory of their civilization. Every major decision, every discovery, every lesson learned was being carefully recorded.

"There's another issue," Miguel said, his voice carrying the weight of recent experience. "The separatist groups."

The room fell silent. It was a problem Theon had been dreading but expecting. Not everyone who responded to his campaign was suited for community life. Some had romantic notions about independence and their own little kingdoms.

"How many now?" he asked.

"It's a mixed situation," Miguel replied, consulting his notes. "We have five major independent settlements on the nearest islands. Two, like the farmers' collective on Westwind, are struggling. Poor crop yields, and they're requesting assistance."

The phrase hung in the air. Everyone understood that assistance might mean sharing their own communal supplies with people who refused to be part of the community.

He paused. "But others are thriving. The Azurath Collective, founded by settlers who wanted to build their own culture, has become a major trading partner. And the logging community at Pine

Ridge now supplies most of our building materials. Not all who leave fail; some simply specialize."

Three-year-old Erik played in the corner of the meeting hall, building structures with carved wooden blocks, then breaking them with a stick, loud roaring, and stomping. Theon watched his son occasionally, feeling the subtle resemblance between this game and their own issues.

"What do the struggling ones specifically want?" Theon asked.

"Food, medical supplies, technical expertise," Miguel reported. "Their spokesman claims their crops failed due to insufficient rain."

Theon caught Helena shaking her head – their own crops thrived in the same weather. "I'd say it's because of poor planning and inadequate soil preparation," she commented.

Settlements usually failed when farmers were too dependent on modern technology – machines, soil meters, irrigation drones. None of it worked on Azoria. Here, they needed hands-on skills, farming knowledge, and patience. Without those, small groups had to rely on hunting alone, but that couldn't sustain them in the long term.

"They thought they could just mimic Liberty Drift," Miguel said. "But paper plans don't teach working with a spade or soil chemistry."

"We provide emergency medical aid," Theon decided. "Anyone seriously ill or injured gets treatment, no questions asked. Basic food supplies to prevent starvation, but not enough to make them rely solely on us."

"And if they refuse to accept help on those terms?" asked Garrett, who had been unusually quiet during the meeting.

"Then we'll reassess," Theon replied, though privately he feared what the reassessment might mean.

After the meeting, as the council members dispersed and Erik went to play outside with other children, Theon stood alone in the empty hall.

It was everything he'd promised in his campaign and more. People worked with their hands, built their own homes, grew their own food. Children played safely while adults collaborated on meaningful projects. The technology was simple, the community bonds strong, the connection to nature profound.

So why did success feel so much like a burden?

Helena approached quietly. "You're not responsible for every decision they make," she said gently.

Theon didn't reply, his face showing he thought otherwise.

She continued, "People make their own choices. You offered them an opportunity. What they do with it is up to them."

Looking through the window at his son playing, Theon thought that all the successes and failures, all the unintended consequences, would shape Erik's life.

"I just hope we're building something worthy of him," Theon murmured.

"We are," Helena said with quiet conviction. "We are."

When Paradise Bleeds

The emergency meeting was called at dawn, but Theon had been awake since the attack. He sat at the head of the council table, staring at the bloodstained shirt Selena had cut away from one of the victims. Three dead, including young Thomas, barely sixteen years old. Five wounded, two fighting for their lives.

"Multiple predators," Selena reported, her usually steady voice tight with strain. "A pack of at least five mountain lions working together. They came through the eastern perimeter where the fence was incomplete."

Theon closed his eyes, fighting the wave of guilt and anger that threatened to overwhelm him. In his marketing materials, he had mentioned the "majestic wildlife" as part of Azoria's appeal. He had made it sound romantic, adventurous – another element of the authentic "ancestral" experience.

He had never mentioned that the majestic wildlife might hunt human children.

"Third attack in two months," Miguel noted grimly. "First livestock, then storage areas, and now people. The ship landings and expanding farms have driven them from their hunting grounds. Now they're returning in packs, desperate and aggressive. There might be more out there."

Helena reached over and squeezed Theon's hand. Seven months pregnant with their second child, she was one of the first to push for better defenses. Theon, however, had resisted this idea because he wanted to preserve the peaceful image that attracted people to their community.

"The eastern perimeter must be completed immediately," he decided, his voice harsh with self-recrimination. "Every available person works on it until it's finished. And we need better protection against these animals."

"Spears and crossbows aren't enough," Garrett said bluntly. He had been adapting various technologies, but was mostly focused on transportation and construction rather than weapons. "I've been working on a compressed air system – basically a rifle that uses mechanical compression. It could be effective against large predators."

Leopold Arkwright shifted uncomfortably. "Developing weapons wasn't part of our original vision."

"Neither was burying children," Theon snapped, immediately regretting his tone but unable to control the anger. "I'm sorry, Leopold. But we're not living in a theoretical paradise anymore. We're trying to survive in a real world with real dangers."

"How long for a working prototype?" Theon asked Garrett.

"Two weeks, maybe less if I can get help with the metalwork."

"Do it," Theon decided. "Whatever you need."

After the meeting, Theon walked alone to the eastern fence line where the attack had occurred. Dark stains on the ground spoke of the violence that had taken place there. Their previous life experience had never suggested they would need fences and protection from the wildlife.

"Daddy!" Erik's voice called, and Theon turned to see his son running toward him with the boundless energy of childhood. Helena followed more slowly, her pregnancy making movement uncomfortable.

"What are you doing out here?" she asked when she caught up.

"Trying to figure out where we went wrong," Theon admitted, lifting his boy.

"We didn't go wrong," Helena said firmly. "We encountered a problem and we're solving it. That's what people do."

Erik pointed toward the forest beyond the fence. "Lions live in the forest," he said seriously. "Mama says they're dangerous."

The simple innocence in his son's voice cut through Theon's brooding. They wanted Erik to grow up surrounded by natural beauty, learning real skills, being part of something authentic. The fact that it came with dangers didn't negate the value.

"Yes, they are dangerous," Theon told his son. "That's why we're building fences and making other plans to keep everyone safe."

"Will you protect us?" Erik asked with the absolute trust that only a child could have.

The weight of that trust – not just from Erik, but from thousands of people living here – settled on Theon's shoulders like a mantle he could never remove.

"Yes," he promised. "Whatever it takes."

That evening, he had an argument with Helena.

He came home late; Erik was already sleeping, and Helena was not in a good mood. "You never come back from work," she said bitterly. "Ever."

He tried to protest, "I do, and I'm here right now!"

"Even now you're still working, still thinking about the council, the fence, responsibility, what-ifs!"

"Helena, children died! I have to make sure it never happens again!" Theon replied.

"And what about your children? When was the last time you spent a day with Erik? Do you even know what his favorite game is? What books does he love?" She was barely holding back from shouting.

"That's not fair! You know I'm doing all of this for you and Erik!"

She cried, "If you're doing this for him, why is there so little of you in his life?"

"Helena, those people rely on me! They're like my children – I brought them here and I just can't abandon them!"

"Even if that means abandoning your family?"

"What do you want from me, Helena?" Theon said tiredly.

"Start an election. Form a government. Let the people decide who's going to be in charge. Let the government solve issues instead of you fixing everything."

Theon didn't respond. She was right – he had taken on too much responsibility and assumed the role of a father for thousands of colonists.

The easy part was over. Now came the real test of whether his vision could survive contact with an unforgiving reality.

From Tools to Weapons

"The steam engine design is solid," Garrett said, spreading blueprints across the workshop table. "Early tests show it can produce enough power for the rotary blades. If we add a fraction of Rational Element for lift, we should get steady, controlled flight."

Before this invention, they had used gliders and balloons to travel between islands. This had significantly limited trade, and distant islands loved playing independent – right up until they needed help.

President Theon looked over the diagrams with a mix of excitement and unease. Ten years after landing, the settlement had grown far beyond anything he had imagined. Their "return to the old ways" had ended up requiring technology that would have seemed impossible when they first arrived.

But those changes were necessary. His campaign was still drawing new settlers every year. Just last week, another ship had docked with three hundred more people chasing the "primitive paradise" he had promised. Across Liberty Drift and its smaller outposts, the population had passed eight thousand.

The economic system had evolved to handle this scale. Specialized workshops produced tools and equipment, while agricultural cooperatives managed food distribution. They had developed a sophisticated barter economy based on work credits and resource allocation councils. Trade with other islands provided materials they couldn't produce locally, creating a complex web of economic relationships.

"Make it a priority," Theon decided. "These airships could revolutionize everything – exploration, trade, communication. We need better ways to coordinate this many people across multiple islands."

"Speaking of other settlements," Miguel interjected, "we have received word from the northern watchtowers. A woman calling herself Captain Lana Mercer has requested a meeting. She claims to represent something called the Red Harvest Collective."

Theon felt the familiar knot of dread tighten in his stomach. Failed settlements turning to raiding had become an increasingly common pattern. Some people had discovered that survival required skills and dedication their previous lives hadn't prepared them for. And desperate people were as dangerous as desperate animals.

"What do we know about this collective?" he asked.

"Very little," Miguel admitted. "Intelligence suggests they're a new group that formed on a northern island cluster. They were originally farmers, but multiple crop failures drove them to desperation."

"And now they're what, exactly?"

"Most likely raiders. They carry weapons and try to look intimidating."

Eleven-year-old Erik looked up from his workbench in the corner, working on some woodworking project. His bright eyes took in the adult conversation with the serious attention that worried Theon. His son was growing up surrounded by discussions of violence and territorial conflicts, while his sister was helping her mother in the garden. This was hardly the childhood the marketing campaign had promised.

"Arrange the meeting," Theon decided. "With full security precautions. Main hall, tomorrow at noon. We'll hear what Captain Mercer has to say before making judgments."

After Miguel left, Garrett rolled up his diagrams with practiced efficiency. "You realize what this pattern means? Armed groups forming from failed settlements, territorial claims hardening, resources becoming scarce… we're heading toward conflicts that will require more than compressed air rifles to resolve."

It stung because Garrett was right, and Theon knew it. Azoria had attracted thousands of people over the past decade. Not all had found the paradise they expected, and some had decided to take what they needed from those who had been more successful.

"I know," Theon replied quietly. "The question is how long we can try to stay isolated and when we should start forming military alliances with nearby settlements."

"And what if we can't tell which settlements share our values until it's too late?"

Theon looked at Erik. "Then we make sure we're strong enough to protect what matters most."

The Price of Justice

The main hall had been designed for community meetings, not as a court, but that's what it had become. Captain Lana Mercer sat in shackles at the defendant's table – the same place where they had first met almost two years ago. Her weathered face showed no remorse for the raids that had terrorized three allied settlements over the past six months.

President Theon sat at the head of the judicial panel, feeling the weight of a decision he had never wanted to make.

"The evidence is clear," Selena Vale, their Chief Medical Officer, reported as medical examiner. "Seven people dead in the raids, including two children. Fifteen injured, several permanently disabled."

Marcus, the Minister of Defense, took the floor next. "The attackers used compressed-air weapons – normally meant for hunting – to terrorize civilian populations. They waited until the harvest was over, then specifically targeted the warehouses. Several raids caused no casualties, but the last one ended in manslaughter."

Theon studied the woman who had once led a successful farming community before successive crop failures drove her people to desperation. They had helped Mercer's community once or twice, supplied seeds and books, signed a trade agreement when she first arrived. But they had resorted to violence anyway.

"Captain Mercer," he said formally, "you led an agricultural settlement of ninety-seven people for three years before turning to raiding. What would justice look like in your opinion?"

Mercer's laugh was bitter. "You want me to beg? To apologize for trying to keep my people alive when your paradise turned out to be a lie?"

The accusation hit like a physical blow. Theon had promised abundance, simplicity, authentic life. For some, those promises had been fulfilled. For others, like Mercer's community, the gap between marketing and reality had proved fatal.

"My people came here because of your grand speeches," Mercer continued, her voice rising. "Work with your hands, live off the land. Well, we tried. We worked until our hands bled, planted crops that failed, watched children starve while you built your perfect little kingdom."

Erik, now thirteen, sat in the observer section, watching his father grapple with the consequences of the campaign that had shaped his entire life. Theon could see the questions in his son's eyes – questions about responsibility, justice, and the price of success.

"The raids you conducted killed innocent people," Theon said, forcing his voice to remain steady. "Including children who never harmed your community."

"And how many children would have died if we had sat on our island waiting for your charity?" Mercer shot back. "At least this way, some of my people survived."

Garrett, Minister of Science and Innovation, presented the evidence with clinical precision. "The weapons used were modified versions of our own designs. Captain Mercer's group acquired the technology through contact with other settlements. The targeting was strategic – food stores, medical supplies, tools. This wasn't random violence but calculated resource acquisition."

After two days of testimony, the panel reached its verdict. Helena and Leopold voted in opposition, but the majority carried the vote.

"Captain Lana Mercer, you are guilty of seven counts of murder, fifteen counts of assault, and multiple counts of armed robbery. Under the laws of the Republic of Liberty Drift, you are sentenced to death by firing squad."

The words felt like poison in Theon's mouth. In twelve years on Azoria, they had never executed anyone. The paradise was supposed to be a place where such choices weren't necessary.

Mercer received the sentence with grim satisfaction. "At least I fought for my people. What did you do? Sat in your tower managing the consequences of your pretty lies."

The execution was carried out three days later. The compressed air rifles Garrett had developed for hunting now served as instruments of justice.

Standing there, Theon felt something fundamental shift inside him. The idealistic marketing specialist who had sold promises of paradise was gone. What remained was a leader who understood that paradise sometimes required terrible choices to preserve it.

The Army

"The population has reached nearly twelve thousand across the main settlement and satellite communities," Miguel reported. The morning briefing had become a daily necessity. "Three more ships arrived last month, but we have received word that the process is slowing down."

Theon nodded grimly. They were all happy that his marketing campaign finally showed signs of slowing down after many years.

The Republic's government had even considered closing the colony to new settlers, hoping to divert them to distant territories. Their nation of colonists and settlers was now considering isolation. Their own children were growing fast and would need valuable space soon.

"Resource allocation?" he asked.

"Stretched but manageable," reported Harlan Wells, who had evolved from a separatist farmer to Minister of Agriculture. "The new territories we have claimed provide additional farmland, but we're approaching the capacity of our lands."

The Republic's success rested on sophisticated resource management systems, governance, and trade.

The colony's population was young and family-oriented. Most settlers had arrived in their twenties and thirties, and the birth rate had climbed to three children per family. Children born on Azoria were becoming adults. Many decided to build homes in the Republic instead of seeking opportunities elsewhere.

"What about organized raiding groups?"

"Increasing," Miguel admitted. "At least three major groups modeled on Mercer's Red Harvest. They're targeting smaller settlements and isolated communities. Some are survivors from failed colonies, others appear to be groups that split off from successful settlements."

The pattern was becoming disturbingly clear. Resources and territories were becoming scarce, territorial claims were hardening, and raiding thrived.

"We need formal alliances," Theon decided. "Schedule diplomatic missions to Eastward Settlement and Azurath. If we're going to protect twelve thousand people, we need partners, not just friends."

"And what about the raiders?" asked Miguel. "Our trading routes are vulnerable. And with Garrett's new zeppelins, they will become even more at risk. Those things are huge and fragile, but can carry tons of cargo and dozens of passengers."

Theon thought that in the early council logs, Garrett's name appeared more than anyone else's. He had developed their engines, flight systems, even tractors – all before Rational Element consumed his every waking thought. But his obsession had borne fruit. Garrett's planes and zeppelins were marvels of steam engineering. They used Rational Element for lift and as a failsafe, but propulsion came from steam engines, needing only wood or coal. The islands had almost no oil – insufficient geological depth for it to form – so combustion engines remained an experiment, far from ready for mass production.

"Suggestions?" he asked.

"President, we need a regular army and a fleet. We have stalled for far too long, but it's time to make this decision."

Theon sighed. He didn't want to militarize the Republic, but there seemed to be no other way. Several more ministers seconded the proposal, and the vote carried by a majority.

That evening, as they walked through the streets of what had become a small city, Helena voiced the worries that weighed on both their minds.

"This isn't what we planned," she said quietly.

"No," Theon agreed. "But I'm not sure what the alternative was. We had to adapt or watch people suffer."

"I know," she said, her hand finding his. "I just worry about what we're building. And what it's costing us."

He understood her concern. Instead of a quiet retirement with a garden and children, they had become the central figures in a civilization. Theon had been re-elected president twice, and it seemed that people saw him as their lifelong leader, despite how he saw himself.

"Erik is growing up too fast," Helena continued. "He's always protesting, pushing back, turning every rule into a fight. He dreams of grand adventures – not just to prove himself, but to escape his father's shadow. I think he's convinced that if he isn't extraordinary, he'll be invisible."

The observation cut deep because it was true. Erik had grown up witnessing tough challenges in governance. He had learned about leadership and sacrifice just by being present for Theon's important decisions. But Theon wasn't sure he wanted such responsibility for his son.

"And Helga?"

"She's more like me – always with the trees, growing plants, testing soil mixes. I won't say she's not ambitious, but at least she's not rebelling. Yet."

They laughed – really laughed – for the first time in a long while.

The Corsair Solution

"The situation with the raiders is escalating," Miguel reported, pointing to red markers scattered across their territorial map. "Captain Redmane's group has moved beyond opportunistic raids to targeting trade routes."

Theon studied the pattern with growing concern. Tomas Redmane had once led a thriving agricultural community on a western island cluster.

"What's their current strength?" he asked.

"Approximately fifteen armed planes of varying sizes," Miguel replied. "They've retrofitted trading craft with compressed air weapons. More concerningly, their coordinated tactics suggest their leadership has military experience."

"We have twice their number of airships. We can fight them if needed," he added.

The transformation of desperate farmers into organized pirates represented everything that could go wrong on Azoria. The constant arrival of new colonists, each bringing different skills, also carried the risk of importing fresh malcontents with every incoming ship.

"They have requested a meeting," Miguel continued. "Redmane claims he wants to negotiate terms for *regulated commerce*."

Leopold shifted uncomfortably in his chair. "Regulated commerce? That's a euphemism for protection payments."

"Most likely," Theon agreed. "But we need to hear what he's offering. Our people depend on those trade routes."

"What if we offered them an alternative to raiding? Legitimate work within the Republic?" asked Helena.

The suggestion was so idealistic that Theon felt a flash of hope, followed immediately by practical concern.

"Pirates don't usually transition to honest labor easily," Leopold said, shaking his head. "Redmane's people have tasted the profits of raiding. Why would they accept lower-paying legitimate work?"

"Because the alternative is eventual destruction," Helena replied. "Raiders succeed by targeting weaker opponents. As settlements organize better defenses and coordinate responses, the raiders face diminishing odds."

"Schedule the meeting," Theon decided. "I want to hear what Redmane actually wants before deciding how to respond."

The meeting took place two days later on Freedom Plateau, an uninhabited island north of Liberty Drift.

Tomas Redmane was younger than Theon had expected – maybe thirty-five – with sharp eyes and the calm confidence of someone shaped by hard circumstances. The way he spoke hinted at a solid education, maybe even a military background.

"President Reeves," Redmane said formally, "thank you for agreeing to this meeting. I know our recent activities have caused concern."

"Your *activities* have cost the Republic significant resources," Theon replied directly. "If there had been any casualties, you would be facing more than just talks," he hinted at Mercer's fate. "What exactly are you proposing?"

Redmane's expression remained serious. "A regulated arrangement. My people control seven key shipping lanes in this region. We're willing to guarantee safe passage for Republic aircraft in exchange for official recognition and mutually beneficial contracts."

"You mean protection payments?"

"I mean a practical solution to a complex problem," Redmane corrected. "Your Republic has grown large enough to attract attention from multiple hostile groups. We're offering to eliminate that threat in exchange for legitimate standing."

Theon studied the man across the table, seeing desperation and pragmatic calculation in equal measure. "What kind of legitimate standing?"

"Incorporation as an autonomous territory within the Republic. We maintain our own governance and security operations, but under the overall authority of Liberty Drift. Think of it as... specialized law enforcement."

The proposal was audacious and potentially brilliant. Instead of fighting an endless series of conflicts with raiders, they could convert the most organized group into allied defenders. The precedent was concerning, but the practical benefits were undeniable.

"You would be willing to operate under our legal framework?"

"Within reason," Redmane replied. "We're not pirates by choice, President Reeves. We're survivors who adapted to the circumstances. Give us a way to survive legitimately, and we'll take it."

After three hours of negotiation, they reached a tentative agreement. Redmane's group would become "Freewind Haven," an autonomous territory specializing in security. They would operate under a formal code of conduct and coordinate with the Republic's authorities on major security threats.

"One final condition," Theon said as they prepared to finalize the terms. "You help us develop that code of conduct. If we're going to legitimize military support, we need rules in place to protect civilians." The message was clear: the raiding had to end.

Redmane nodded, extending his hand. "Agreed. And President Reeves? Thank you for seeing past what we became to what we could be."

Back home on Liberty Drift, Theon reflected on the strange turn his life had taken. They had been on the brink of conflict, but had fortunately averted it through negotiations.

"Do you think it will work?" Helena asked.

"I think desperate people with few options make dangerous enemies – and potentially valuable allies," Theon said. "The real question is how they'll act once they are no longer desperate."

He looked at the horizon, where Redmane's planes were already patrolling, and wondered what would come next. More conflicts? Wars?

Every solution seemed to create new problems. Every decision led to more decisions. The agreement had turned enemies into valuable allies. He hoped he would not regret it.

The Last Garden

The fever took Helena quickly. Ten days from the first symptoms to the end, despite everything Selena and the medical team could do. The pneumonia had started as a simple cold, aggravated by exhaustion from managing the spring planting. Their antibiotics, degraded after decades, proved useless.

"If the Federation ship had arrived just a week earlier…" Selena muttered, staring at the list of failed treatments. "We could have saved her with a single pill."

At forty-seven, Theon had expected many more years with the woman who had been his moral compass, his emotional anchor, and his partner in building a civilization.

Now he stood alone in their bedroom, holding the simple drawing she had made twenty years ago of a floating island with a tree and a waterfall. The paper was worn from handling, the lines faded, but it remained the purest expression of the dream they had shared before reality complicated everything.

The funeral filled Liberty Plaza, the heart of what had grown from their original settlement into the capital. Representatives from allied territories attended, along with nearly a thousand residents of Liberty Drift itself. Helena had touched all their lives through her work, her gentle counsel, and her unwavering support of community values.

"Helena Tordson believed in this world's potential," Theon said, his voice carrying across the silent crowd. "She saw beauty in challenges, hope in setbacks, and possibility in problems. Her gardens still feed us, her research still guides us, her wisdom still shapes our decisions."

Leopold Arkwright spoke next, his voice thick with emotion as he detailed Helena's contributions to their growing body of knowledge. Her botanical research, preserved in the Library, would help future generations understand Azoria's unique ecosystem.

As the ceremony ended and people dispersed, Theon felt an emptiness inside him. He loved his children, felt obligated to his people, and was devoted to his work. But Helena had made it all meaningful.

Erik and Helga stood nearby, their eyes red from tears. Erik was now twenty years old, and Helga was seventeen. Theon realized that his children's connection to their mother was much stronger than their connection to him. He was rarely present, spending most of his time solving Republic problems.

"I'll be traveling to the Heights soon, Father," Erik said. His voice was steady, his resolve clear.

Theon felt a flicker of pride. "The Heights are harsh, Erik. Cold, thin air, and barely enough space to support a settlement. Nobody lives there for a reason. Only the giant eagles like it up there."

"It's more than just exploring," Erik argued. "I've been studying the original survey data from the Library. The electromagnetic interference isn't uniform. The models suggest it's weaker at higher altitudes. If we can establish an outpost in the Heights, we could create a communication window. We could intercept incoming colony ships before their communications are fried. We could send word back about what we really need – proper medical supplies, specific components."

He stopped abruptly, and Theon realized his son was thinking of obtaining the medications that could have saved Helena, blaming himself for not trying this sooner. "It's a long shot, but it's our only chance to break the silence."

Theon stepped closer, placing a hand on Erik's shoulder. "You have my support, son. She would have been proud of you."

That night, alone in the bed he had shared with Helena for more than two decades, Theon stared at the ceiling and tried to imagine the years ahead. Decisions without her counsel. Challenges without her wisdom. Life without her voice.

For the first time since his youth, Theon felt truly alone.

The Friend and the Enemy

"The experiment was a disaster," Garrett admitted, his blue-stained hands shaking as he placed the preliminary report on Theon's desk. Dark circles under his eyes spoke of days spent in the laboratory, trying to understand what had gone wrong. "Complete destabilization. The island fell within minutes."

Theon read the casualty numbers with growing horror. Twenty-three people had died, and a research outpost was destroyed when an experimental Rational Element extraction caused an island to collapse.

"You assured me this was a controlled test," Theon said, his voice dangerously quiet. Anger and grief competed in his chest — anger at the needless deaths, grief for the families destroyed by his friend's obsession. "On an uninhabited islet, with minimal staff. How did it go this wrong?"

"The preliminary extraction proceeded exactly according to calculations," Garrett explained. "But the way the remaining Rational Element lost its energy – it happened faster than any of our models had predicted."

Theon closed the report, unable to read more casualty details. "Twenty-three families will bury their loved ones because of this *miscalculation*."

"Don't you think I understand that?" Garrett snapped, a rare display of emotion cracking his composure. "But this research is too important to abandon because of setbacks. The potential for

unlimited power, for controlling the very forces that keep us
floating–"

"Listen to yourself," Theon interrupted, standing abruptly.
"You're calling it a *setback*. You're talking about unlimited power
as if it justifies anything."

The accusation hung between them like a physical barrier. For
more than two decades, they'd been friends, collaborators, partners
in building a civilization. Now Theon saw something new in
Garrett's eyes: utter indifference to the human lives lost. For years,
Garrett had been growing more isolated, more obsessed. Theon
remembered Helena's warnings about his friend's changing
behavior, concerns he had dismissed as overwork. The Rational
Element research had consumed him slowly, like an addiction.

"The research continues," Garrett said firmly. "Under stricter
protocols, with better safety measures, but it continues. We're too
close to breakthrough discoveries to stop now."

"No," Theon said with absolute finality. "All Rational Element
research is suspended. Indefinitely. We need your resources
elsewhere."

Garrett's face flushed with anger. "You can't do that. This is
bigger than your authority, bigger than any political concerns. The
Plan should proceed! This research could reshape everything –
transportation, construction, trade."

"The decision has already been made," Theon replied, feeling
that something was deeply wrong with his friend and his obsession.
"This needs to stop."

"And if I refuse?"

The question carried implications that neither man wanted to
articulate. This wasn't Garrett who had helped build their first

shelters, who had laughed with them around campfires. The Rational Element had become an addiction.

"Then you'll be relocated to the Drifts, where your research obsessions can't endanger innocent people," Theon said quietly. "Don't make me choose between your friendship and the safety of the Republic, Garrett. You won't like my decision."

After Garrett left, Theon stood alone in his office, staring at Helena's drawing, pain gripping his heart. What would she have advised? How would she have handled a friend corrupted by ambition?

The answer came with painful clarity: she would have seen this moment coming years earlier and found a way to redirect Garrett's obsessions before they became dangerous.

Theon had missed the signs of his friend's transformation. Now he faced the consequences of that oversight.

Six months later, reports reached Liberty Drift that Garrett had displaced a governor in the Drifts with the help of several sympathizers. Intelligence suggested he was now offering technological secrets to smaller settlements in exchange for resources and loyalty.

"He's building a power base," Miguel reported during an emergency council session. "Using his expertise to attract followers who feel marginalized by the Republic's success."

Theon studied the regional map, noting the locations where Garrett had been reported. A pattern was emerging – settlements with failed crops, political disputes, or resource shortages. Places where people might be desperate enough to overlook moral questions in favor of promised solutions.

"He knows exactly what he's doing," Selena observed grimly. "He's targeting communities with grievances against us, offering them the power to level the playing field."

"Worse," Leopold added, "he has detailed knowledge of our defenses, our resources, and our political relationships. He helped design many of our systems."

Erik, now twenty-three and preparing for a second expedition to the Heights, spoke up from his position near the back of the room. "What if we're approaching this wrong? Instead of trying to contain Garrett, what if we addressed the grievances he's exploiting?"

It was exactly the kind of question Helena would have asked – focusing on root causes rather than symptoms, seeking understanding rather than conflict.

"Some grievances can't be addressed through diplomacy," Theon replied, though he hated the hardness in his own voice. "Some people want power more than they want justice, and they'll use any excuse to justify taking what they want."

The room fell silent.

"Find him," Theon ordered Miguel. "Before he turns our own innovations against us."

The Unification Wars

"The eastern coalition has secured the Windward Approaches," Miguel reported, pointing to blue markers on the strategy map that now dominated Theon's situation room. "Garrett's forces have withdrawn to defensive positions around their main base in the Drifts."

Theon nodded, studying the map with the eye of a commander – a role he had never imagined for himself when he first envisioned their escape to a simpler world. The "Unification Wars," as historians would later call them, had consumed three years of his life and transformed their society.

"Casualties?" he asked.

"Lighter than projected. The pressure tactics worked – most settlements surrendered rather than endure a prolonged siege. Garrett's core supporters are now isolated on seven islands in the Drifts archipelago."

The war had begun when Garrett had used his Rational Element research to destabilize a floating island that had refused to join his so-called Kingdom of the Drifts. Watching the entire community fall into the storm below had convinced Theon that diplomacy was no longer an option.

The Republic's economic advantages had proved decisive. Their production systems and warehouses had switched to producing planes and weapons with ease. There was no need for large-scale ground operations, so civilian life remained relatively undisturbed. Garrett's alliance of desperate settlements lacked the organizational infrastructure for prolonged conflict.

"Supply lines from the northern allies remain secure," Miguel continued. "Admiral Redmane's fleet has been surprisingly effective at keeping trade routes open."

Theon suppressed a bitter smile at the title. Tomas Redmane had once been a pirate captain, driven to raiding by desperation. Now he commanded a legitimate force under license from the Republic – a reminder that even outlaws could become allies.

"Timeline for the final phase?" Theon asked.

"Two months, maybe three. Garrett's islands don't have the resources for a prolonged siege. And his support is slipping – people are beginning to see that his promises of unlimited power were nowhere close."

After the briefing, Theon stayed alone in the situation room, surrounded by maps of the world they had reshaped. Blue markers showed settlements under the Republic's protection or alliance. Red marked Garrett's fading territory. Green represented neutral communities that had refused to choose a side.

The blue markers vastly outnumbered the red now, but the cost had been immense. Hundreds dead. Communities displaced. Technology redirected toward warfare. The peaceful Republic Helena had once dreamed of had become something closer to an empire – held together not just by ideals, but by necessity and strategic force.

Victory seemed inevitable, yet Theon felt no triumph. Too many sacrifices. Too many compromises. He had become the kind of leader he once feared: one who justified hard choices in the name of a greater good.

A knock pulled him from his thoughts. Erik entered – now twenty-six, lean, and weathered from years spent in the Heights.

After six years of patient work, starting with orphaned chicks and adapting old falconry techniques from the Library's texts, he had succeeded in taming the giant eagles.

"Reconnaissance confirms Miguel's report," he said. "Garrett's forces are concentrated but demoralized. Even some of his supporters are questioning whether this war was worth it."

Theon looked at his son, noting the restrained judgment in his tone. Unlike his father, Erik had never given up on diplomacy.

"You think I should offer surrender terms?" Theon asked.

"I think you should offer peace," Erik said. "End the fighting. Address the real concerns that led people to follow Garrett. Start rebuilding instead of conquering."

It was exactly what Helena would have said – moral clarity wrapped in practical advice. But Helena had never watched whole islands crumble. She had never had to weigh lives against ideals.

"Garrett gave up the right to negotiate when he started destroying settlements," Theon replied. "Some threats have to be ended, not managed."

Erik was silent for a moment. Then he said the words that would haunt Theon for years:

"Then be sure to write it down – for the generations to come, when they ask why you became the very thing you came to Azoria to escape."

The war would soon be over. Garrett would fall. The Republic would be safe. People would have a chance to build the lives Theon had promised.

But the cost would never stop weighing on him.

Empty Victory

"The Republic is stable," Miguel reported during what had become a routine morning briefing. "Trade routes are safe. All territories recognize regional boundaries. Resource production is higher than consumption throughout the dominion."

Theon nodded, though the words rang hollow. At fifty-seven, he had achieved everything he could ever have wished for – and more. The Republic of Westward Drifts now governed the entire floating world, with over twenty thousand people across dozens of floating islands and subject nations. It covered only a fraction of the planet, but Theon felt it was more than enough. Prosperity, security, technological progress, and well-functioning institutions – they had it all.

So why did success feel so much like failure?

"Population growth has stabilized," Miguel continued. "Immigration from Federation colonies is now minimal, and no new ships are expected. Maria reports that the backlist is now empty. Most newcomers are family members of existing residents, not strangers responding to recruitment."

Census records showed that natural births now accounted for sixty percent of annual population growth. The first generation of Azoria-born citizens totaled three thousand.

After about three decades, his marketing campaign had finally run its course. The great exodus it had sparked was over.

"What about the Heights outpost?" Theon asked, though the question carried more weight than his voice revealed.

"A moderate success," Miguel replied. "They now have a permanent settlement in the Heights – eighty-two people on three connected islands. Reliable glider and eagle transit. They cleared one island entirely and laid out a huge message with stones for incoming ships. They successfully arranged for critical medical supplies. The shipment arrived with the last colony vessel – it's already saved lives."

Erik, now thirty, had spent the last ten years creating what Theon once dreamed of: a small community focused on human connection instead of bureaucracy. It was everything the *Return to Your Roots* campaign had promised, achieved by a man who had grown up watching its failure to scale.

"Erik requested permission to expand," Miguel added. "He believes the Heights could support several hundred people, given the right organization."

Theon felt that familiar ache – pride tangled with loss. Erik was living his father's dream, not by fulfilling it, but by rejecting the system it had become. And with each success, each report of lives saved through his son's work, Theon felt the distance between them growing wider.

Later, Theon walked through Liberty Drift's administrative district. Where there had once been communal meeting circles, there were now formal government halls. Informal exchanges had given way to complex economic structures. Consensus had yielded to hierarchical governance.

It was stable. It was efficient. It was nothing like what Helena had imagined.

At Unity Plaza, surrounded by memorial stones from the Unification Wars, Theon tried to remember the last time he had felt genuinely happy. Erik's birth? The day they landed? Helga's first steps?

Everything since had been duty. Expectations. Leadership. He had become a father to twenty thousand people who believed in his vision – at the cost of growing distant from the family he actually had. Helga was already married and living in a small agricultural colony on Border Drift. He felt she despised the man he had become. They hadn't talked in years, not since the war.

A courier approached, handing him an envelope.

Father – We've built something remarkable here. A place where people know each other, where work means something, where children grow up in tune with the world instead of lost in complexity. We are riding giant eagles now, soaring between the islands in Heights as our ancestors sailed the seas. It's what Mother dreamed of.

I know your responsibilities make it hard to leave, but I want you to know – you weren't wrong. Just too successful. If you ever want to lay that burden down, there's room for you here. Among dozens of friends, not thousands of subjects.

Your son, Erik

Theon felt something breaking loose in his chest. Erik was offering him a way out – an escape from the weight of his own creation. A chance to finally live the life he'd sold to others but never claimed for himself.

But could he walk away from twenty thousand people who depended on him? Could he step back from a world that only held together because of his persistence?

"I see the cage," Theon told Helena's drawing that evening. "Bars built from promises I made to too many people."

Success could be the cruelest failure of all, when it trapped you in something you'd never really wanted.

When Everything Burns

The sharp smell of smoke filled the air as Theon neared the Library, his heart pounding as he saw the orange glow lighting the night sky. Fire engines with steam pumps were already at work, their crews aiming water at the burning building that had been the heart of their civilization for thirty-four years.

"What happened?" he asked Leopold's successor, a middle-aged woman whose tears reflected the flames.

"Started in the preservation wing," she replied, her voice choked with emotion. "The official word is an oil lamp accident, but it spread too quickly, Theon. Far too quickly. It was as if it had been planned to cause maximum damage. Chief Librarian Fontaine is still inside…"

Theon stared in horror at the building that contained thirty-four years of accumulated knowledge. Books brought from their original worlds. Detailed records of every discovery they had made on Azoria. Helena's botanical research. The complete history of their civilization's development. It was more than a building; it was the institutional memory of everything they had accomplished.

And now flames were consuming it all.

There were enough Garrett sympathizers around, and people overall who thought that he had overstayed as president for far too long. Someone might have decided to fulfill their revenge by hitting his weakest point.

"Where is Fontaine exactly?" he asked.

"Central archive chamber. He went back after the first evacuation to rescue the historical documents and the original Earth texts."

Theon started toward the building, but strong hands held him back.

"You can't go in, sir," a fire captain said firmly. "The roof is about to collapse. It's too dangerous."

As if to prove his point, a thunderous crash came from inside the building, followed by a fresh burst of sparks shooting into the night sky. Part of the eastern wing collapsed inward, sending burning debris cascading down.

Theon watched helplessly as the firefighters battled flames they couldn't defeat. The Library's contents – paper, leather, wood – were perfect fuel for destruction. The fire had too much of a head start.

By dawn, the devastation was complete. The Library stood as a smoldering ruin, with only parts of the walls showing the original structure. Chief Librarian Julien Fontaine hadn't emerged from the building.

Theon thought, with a touch of bitterness, that it was for the best Leopold Arkwright had died last year. The old man might have had a heart attack watching his life's work go up in flames.

Theon stood among the ashes, looking at the destruction that felt like more than the loss of a building. Here lay the accumulated wisdom that existed nowhere else, preserved only in memories that would fade with the people who held them.

"More than seventy percent of the collection is gone," reported the fire captain, his face streaked with soot and exhaustion. "Half of the rest suffered water damage."

Seventy percent. The number hit Theon like a physical blow. Decades of knowledge reduced to ash overnight.

As he turned to leave the ruins, Theon noticed a partially burned book in the debris. Kneeling carefully, he recognized one of Helena's botanical journals, its delicate drawings of Azorian plants now charred and water-damaged.

He lifted it gently, this fragment of his wife's legacy, feeling the weight of loss multiply. Helena had died fourteen years ago, but her work had kept part of her alive for him. Now, even that connection was severed.

At sixty-one, having led their community for over three decades, Theon had built his legacy on the cornerstone of preserved knowledge. The Library's destruction felt like judgment, a reminder of how fragile even the most solid achievements could be.

Walking slowly back to the administrative complex, still holding Helena's journal, Theon began to think seriously about stepping down. The weight of others' dreams, the burden of responsibilities he'd never asked for – suddenly, it all felt like too much.

It was time for a change – not just for the Republic, but for himself.

A Message from the Heights

Two years after the fire, Theon was reviewing morning reports when the emergency courier arrived. The young messenger's face was pale as he handed over a sealed letter marked *urgent*.

The message was from the Heights:

President Reeves – It is my duty to tell you that your son Erik died yesterday during an eagle-riding expedition. The accident happened during a routine flight to survey new settlement sites.

According to witnesses, Erik's eagle suddenly lost altitude during the approach to a landing platform. Despite Erik's attempts to regain control, the bird struck the platform edge and the rider fell. He plummeted into the Depths below. The body was never recovered.

Erik died doing what he loved, leading people toward the life that your family has always championed. His loss is felt deeply by everyone in the Heights community.

With deepest sympathy,
Skyra Nordman,
Acting Settlement Coordinator

Theon read the message three times before the words fully sank in. Erik, his beloved son, was gone. He had been Theon's connection to the original dream, the only person living the authentic life Theon had promised.

The weight of loss was crushing. Erik had been thirty-six years old, in the prime of his life, leading a small community. He had tamed eagles, built a thriving settlement, and lived a peaceful life without the wars and politics that consumed his father.

Miguel found him hours later, still sitting at his desk with the message in his hands.

"Sir?" Miguel said gently. "The afternoon council meeting–"

"Cancel it," Theon said without looking up. "Cancel everything for the rest of the week."

"Of course, sir. Is there anything–"

"My son is dead, Miguel," Theon said quietly. "Erik fell from his eagle yesterday."

Miguel's sharp intake of breath was the only sound in the room for a long moment. Then, softly: "I'm so sorry, sir. Erik was… he was special. He understood things that most of us never quite grasped."

Theon nodded, unable to speak. Erik truly had Helena's vision of life and success – something Theon had always lacked.

"What would you like me to tell the council?" Miguel asked.

"Tell them I need time to think," Theon replied. "About succession, about the Heights, about what comes next."

After Miguel left, Theon looked out the window at Liberty Drift's busy streets. Thousands of people were going about their lives, building families and businesses. They deserved leadership, stability, the continued prosperity that his governance had provided.

Theon found himself wondering whether his responsibilities would ever end.

That night, alone in the house that had once echoed with Helena's laughter and their children's games, Theon finally made a decision that had been building for years.

He thought of his daughter Helga, living quietly on Border Drift. After the Library fire, he had reached out to her, hoping to reconnect. She had responded quickly and sharply. She wanted nothing to do with "a tyrant who betrayed everything her mother dreamed of."

The words still stung, but he understood them now. Both of his children had seen what his success had cost.

It was time. Time to honor his family's memory by living the dream instead of just managing its consequences.

The Return

"The balloon's ready," announced the captain, checking the final preparations on a craft that would carry Theon to the Heights.

A small crowd had gathered to watch him leave, though Theon had asked for no ceremony. Miguel stood at the front, already showing the weight of his new role as Acting President of the Republic until the next election. The transition had been planned for months, ensuring the government would continue functioning while Theon finally pursued the life he had promised but never lived.

"The Republic will remember your service," Miguel said formally, offering his hand. "Skyward Theon, founder and unifier."

The title still sounded strange to Theon–"Skyward Theon" was his historical name now, the one future generations would use. It captured his success and the bitter truth: he had united the sky islands but never found peace among them.

"Remember why we came here," Theon replied quietly, shaking Miguel's hand. "Freedom, cooperation, the chance to build something real. Don't let bureaucracy hide the purpose."

With final goodbyes to old friends and colleagues, Theon boarded the balloon. Fourteen volunteers came with him – people who also yearned for the simple life that had been lost in their success.

As the ground crew released the ropes and the balloon rose steadily, Theon felt a lightness that had nothing to do with the lift. For the first time in decades, he was moving toward something he wanted.

The middle-altitude islands grew smaller as they rose toward the Heights. Looking down, Theon could see what they had built: busy towns connected by trade routes, clear borders, and strong systems that kept twenty thousand people safe and comfortable.

It was everything his campaign had promised, only bigger. It was a copy of the Federation, only smaller.

No wonder he had felt so unhappy as their leader.

"Look," called one of his companions, pointing ahead. "The Heights!"

Through the thin air, Theon saw it – a cluster of small islands. Some were linked by bridges and walkways, others trailing waterfalls into the clouds. Children practiced sky navigation in gliders while giant eagles soared overhead.

As they approached the landing platform, Theon spotted a middle-aged woman waiting with other settlers. This was Skyra, the one who had informed him of Erik's death. Now she led the community his son had built.

The balloon touched down softly, and Theon stepped onto solid ground that felt more like home than anywhere he'd been since Helena died. Skyra came forward with a smile full of quiet understanding.

"Welcome to the Heights," she said simply. "Welcome home."

Looking at the small group who had built something real in this high, quiet place, Theon felt peace settle over him like a blanket. This was the life he had once promised to others: meaningful work, nature all around, and freedom.

He had finally reached his dream, just three and a half decades late.

Full Circle

Elder Theon sat on the worn stone bench outside his simple Heights home, watching the morning routine of the eagle riders. At sixty-eight, his body was frail, but his mind stayed sharp, holding the wisdom of a lifetime spent building, leading, and finally finding peace.

The Windclaw Tribe – Erik's community – had grown strong on its own over the past years. Theon had never claimed leadership, letting the community develop its own culture and traditions. Many customs were inspired by Helena's Norse stories but adapted to fit life in the Heights.

Theon found deep meaning in this final chapter of his life. After decades of constant stress, the peaceful rhythm of tribal life restored something he had lost. He had tried eagle riding, though age now kept him from long trips. Mostly, he watched the younger generation thrive in ways he had only dreamed possible.

"The wind patterns are shifting," said Skyra, approaching with her usual keen observation. Her skill with the eagles matched Erik's, and she could read the weather almost like magic.

Theon nodded, watching the great eagles. These birds were magnificent, and the tribe's close bond with them showed how humans could adapt in beautiful ways.

"Storm coming?" he asked.

"More likely prey movement on the western islands," Skyra answered, watching the birds closely. "They can sense things we cannot."

They sat quietly, watching the young riders prepare. This generation saw the Republic below as distant and overly complicated, preferring the direct connection to the sky and wind.

Sometimes, Theon found the perspective almost amusing. The Republic he had built was too large, too organized, too far removed from real human life. He had been right to leave it – even if it had been far too late.

"Message from below," said a young courier, handing Theon a sealed letter from the regular balloon delivery.

Theon recognized Miguel's handwriting on the seal. As he read it, his expression grew serious.

"News?" asked Skyra.

"Miguel is stepping down as President due to health issues," Theon said. "The Council has chosen Amara Chen's grandson to lead now." He continued reading. "They also rebuilt part of the Library. Not as large as before, but functioning."

Skyra nodded. She knew this mattered to Theon, even if it felt distant from their life now. "Will you respond?"

"Later," he said, folding the message. "The hunting party comes first."

They walked to the launch platform, where the riders checked their equipment. Eagle riding required specialized gear – saddles, safety equipment – all crafted from local materials but based on sound engineering.

Theon watched with pride as the young hunters prepared. Their world was simple – eagle riding, tribal customs, and shared traditions. Yet they were not primitive, just free from outside control and closer to nature.

As the eagles lifted off into the vast sky, Theon smiled with a quiet joy he had missed for most of his life.

"Your son built something special," Skyra said, watching the hunters disappear.

"Erik succeeded where I failed," Theon replied. "He knew the dream was right – but the scale was wrong. You can't sell paradise to thousands. You build it with a few."

That evening, in his quiet home, Theon sat beside Helena's old drawing. It hung on the wall next to tribal artwork. He began writing a letter to Miguel. His hand was unsteady, but his thoughts were clear:

Miguel – Congratulations on a successful transition. The Republic is stronger than any one leader, which was always the plan. Erik's work here continues to flourish, proving the original dream wasn't wrong – just misunderstood. When people ask about the early days, remind them that every dream worth chasing needs both ambition and humility. The Heights teach us that some things are more beautiful when they remain small.

Your friend, Theon

As he sealed the letter for tomorrow's courier, Theon reflected on his journey. He had spent three and a half decades building a world that could function without him, and now spent his final years learning to live without the world he built.

He took a drawing from the frame, folded it, and put it into his pocket.

His campaign had changed the world. It had given people a better life. But this – this quiet, authentic life with others who chose it – that was the true success.

As sleep came, with only the wind and eagle cries in the background instead of meetings and regulations, Theon felt a kind of ease he hadn't known since Helena's death.

In his final moment, Theon reached for Helena's drawing one last time. He smiled, remembering two young dreamers planning their escape to paradise.

They had found it, in the end. Just not the way they expected.

The drawing fluttered gently as Theon's breath slowed and stopped. Elder Theon – once Theon Reeves, marketing expert, president, now a quiet tribesman – had finally reached peace.

History would remember him as Skyward Theon, the unifier, the founder of a Republic that lasted over three hundred years. His ideas and culture would shape the middle altitudes for generations.

But in the end, he was just a man who learned that the simplest dreams were the most powerful ones.

ALEX O. HARB
THE
SQUEAKING
GATE

THE SQUEAKING GATE

She left.

Oliver stood in the front garden, rain soaking through his shirt, staring at the gate she had slammed behind her. He could see her figure disappearing down the street. The gate's iron bars still shivered from the force of the slam.

He couldn't remember how the fight had started. It was something about his work that he ignored, as usual. He waited for her to calm down, but instead, she took the suitcase already sitting in the hallway and stormed out the front door. He followed her outside into the rain, trying to tell her that the work of his life was on the verge of a breakthrough or collapse, but she wouldn't listen.

"We have no friends anymore, Oliver! No life! When was the last time we dined together? When did we last go anywhere?" Her words had cut deeper than any blade. And the most unsettling part was that she was now calm and determined. "You haven't spoken to me – really spoken – in weeks. It's like living with a ghost. I won't take it anymore."

But it was her final words, as she wrenched the gate open, that echoed loudest: "You don't even have time to fix the fucking gate!"

The gate squeaked as usual, demanding extra force to open.

The gate. His childhood masterpiece, his first engineering triumph. A counterweight moved in the welded tube, shutting the gate closed – now jamming and squeaking every other time. Thirteen years since he built it to guard himself from the *outside*, from the world he dreaded so much.

The memories of recent months flooded back as he stood there by the gate.

The Royal Minister's voice rang in his ears: "Your refined oil is impressive, Mr. Luber, but the Kingdom needs practical applications." The man had toured their laboratory with barely masked impatience. "We cannot wait indefinitely for you to solve this ignition problem. We need the engines you promised, or we are shutting down the project."

His superior's frustration had grown more visible each day. "Another failure! The heated metal rods cool too quickly, and these chemical igniters are a dead end…" The man stomped around the lab in anger. "We are so close! Luber, it was your idea – now you need to make it work!"

And her voice, from what felt like a lifetime ago: "Oliver, you are barely sleeping! You can't hide inside forever with your calculations! The world won't wait while you finish your work!" She had begged him to join her for simple pleasures – a walk, a meal at the tavern, anything beyond these four walls. "I miss who you were. I miss us."

He could have told her the truth – that every time he passed through that gate, every venture into the outside world required a small act of courage. That the world beyond the gate felt like enemy territory. That even going with her for dinner meant forcing himself through anxiety.

But he never had time to explain.

The rain soaked through his shirt as he leaned against the slightly warm tube with the counterweight. It was always warm, even in winter. He had noticed it as a child but never questioned it.

Memory washed over him: ten years old, watching his uncle arrive with a metal tube six feet long. "Waste piece from the shipyard," Uncle had said, ruffling Oliver's hair. "Perfect for that gate mechanism idea of yours – but welded shut at one end."

As a child, he had been so afraid of the outside – the dreaded destinations beyond the gate were subjects of his nightmares. It got better with the mechanism, which kept the door closed and his anxiety at bay.

Even then, freshly built and properly lubricated, the tube had grown warm during use. Young Oliver had often pressed his palm against the bottom, marveling at the heat. He had assumed it was just friction from the moving weight.

But now, thinking of the mechanism, he suddenly understood: the counterweight wasn't just sliding in the tube – it was compressing the air trapped at the bottom. Rapid compression of air in an enclosed space. And rapid compression created…

Heat. Intense heat.

His breath caught as the revelation struck him. If you compress air quickly enough, in a small enough space, it might heat to temperatures that could ignite fuel. No heated rods. No chemical primers. Just compression. Pure, simple, mechanical compression.

Their refined oil would ignite beautifully in air heated by rapid compression. A piston driving down in a cylinder, compressing the air until it reached ignition temperature, then injecting the fuel at the precise moment…

The solution had been here all along, built by his own hands.

———

Five years later, Oliver stood at the same gate. His white shirt was crisp, his black cylinder and formal attire a sharp contrast to the rusted iron. He tugged at the knot of his black tie for the thousandth time and reached into his jacket pocket to touch the letter. It was written in elegant script on heavy paper, and he had read it countless times:

> *By Royal Decree, in recognition of your contributions to engine technology and your invaluable service to the Kingdom of Tides, you are hereby invited to accept induction into the Royal Academy of Sciences as its youngest member, and to receive the honor of knighthood...*

The compression engine had changed everything. Trains powered by his invention could haul hundreds of carriages. Horseless carriages were entering production. Even engines for flying machines were in development.

Yet the familiar tightness crept into his chest. The world awaited – crowds of dignitaries, speeches, ceremonies. All the recognition he had dreamed of required him to venture through his gate. *Outside.*

The gate squeaked exactly as it had five years ago – he had never found the time to oil it properly. But this time, the mechanism jammed completely. Years of corrosion had finally seized the counterweight system.

Oliver pulled harder, then pushed. The ceremony would begin in an hour. He couldn't disappoint the Royal Academy. He couldn't miss his moment of triumph.

He threw his full weight against the gate.

Something snapped inside the tube with a sharp crack. The heavy chain that had held the counterweight for eighteen years parted and shot from the top of the tube like a whip and landed on Oliver's temple.

He collapsed instantly, his white shirt staining with blood. The knighthood ceremony invitation fluttered from his pocket, landing beside the gate that had given him everything – and taken it all back.

———

Professor Heinrich Marlowe, Oliver's former superior, received the knighthood that autumn. In his acceptance speech, he briefly mentioned the promising junior researcher who had contributed to the compression ignition before his tragic accident.

Oliver Luber's name still made it into history, though not as he might have hoped. When people spoke of maintaining machinery, of the importance of proper care and lubrication, they would say they needed "to luber" the mechanism.

It was a fitting legacy for a man who dreaded the world beyond the gate. In the end, what he feared most didn't come from *outside* – it came from *within*.

ALEX O. HARB

STEAMROBBERS

STEAMROBBERS

The barman stood at the bar, polishing a glass as he heard the sound of a landing steam plane.

Patrons quieted for a moment.

"Waiting for someone?" asked one.

"Nah, mail zeppelin is next month," replied the barman.

They had little to no guests here on the frontier. Rare supply runs were their only communication to the big world.

After a while, a man in a fancy suit and cylinder hat came in. He looked around with a look of disdain on his aristocratic face. "Whiskey," he ordered, "on the rocks." The barman silently pointed to a sign behind him: **NO ICE EVER!**

The man cursed and added, "Whiskey and a glass of water, then."

The barman poured him a shot and a glass of water from the pitcher. "Two coins for whiskey, five for water."

"Are you insane?" exploded the man. "Why the hell does water cost more than whiskey?"

"It's the frontier," the barman explained dryly. "Take it or leave it."

The man cursed once again, took off his white gloves, and counted the coins. He sat in the corner, sipping his whiskey.

Patrons returned to their talks. "… and that classy engineer said, *'There should be some water underground!'* They brought fancy long tubes and started drilling north of the ridge, where that single tree grows. And you know what? They drilled and drilled, put tube after tube into the ground!"

"And what then? They found water?"

"Hell, no! They drilled clean through the bloody island! The tubes started falling down, swooshing, and taking the drill and other fancy equipment they had! They watched that hole with a dot of blue sky underneath and left."

Laughter rose from around the bar. Everyone knew there was no water on this floating island. Nobody was that stupid to drill too deep – the best ore deposits were at the ridge shallows.

In a few minutes, the pilot entered the bar. He looked around and went to the aristocrat's table. "Sir, we're out of water for the steam engine."

"Then find a bloody well."

"There is no well in the village. No maintenance station, no nothing," replied the pilot. "Only sand!"

At this moment, three masked figures entered the bar. They had handkerchiefs hiding their faces and guns in their hands.

"Everybody, don't move! It's a robbery!"

The leader pointed his gun at the man in the cylinder hat. The aristocrat started rambling: "You don't know who I am! I won't tolerate such behavior! I have money and connections!"

"Don't care about your money – it's of no value here," snapped the robber and took the glass from the aristocrat's table. Another one took the canteen from the pilot's belt. The robbers carried several metal canisters painted green. They started walking around the bar, pouring water from glasses and water bottles into the canisters.

"You," the leader pointed his gun at the barman, "what do you have?"

The barman obediently put three pitchers and a big sealable can on the bar. The robbers poured it all and disappeared.

The bar was silent for a moment, but then exploded with curses.

"How are we supposed to live until the next supply without water?"

"At least there's some whiskey left," the barman replied.

The aristocrat tried complaining, asked for a sheriff and a mayor, but there were none on the island.

After a while, he said to the pilot, "Damn it. We're leaving."

"Sir, we can't leave. We don't have a drop of water in the steam tank. Our plane won't fly without it. We need any liquid. But not whiskey – it's flammable."

"Barman, do you have anything non-flammable? I'll pay double!"

"Nope. Everything's taken or already in the bladders of those gentlemen," the barman made a wide gesture, meaning the patrons. "You'll need to wait until next month."

"Bladders… Pilot, can it fly on piss?" the desperate aristocrat came up with an idea.

The pilot grimaced. "It can, but it'll smell, and we'll need maintenance afterward."

"I don't care! All of you, fill the bucket!" he tried to command the patrons.

Nobody moved. "That's our liquid. We paid for it!" said one voice.

"Bloody hell! I'll pay whatever the cost. Do it!"

———

The barman in a nice black cylinder hat was polishing a glass, looking out the window as a plane coughed out smelly fumes and took flight. He shook his head, put the glass away, and poured a pitcher of water from a nice green canister.

He said to himself, "Frontier ain't no place for arrogant pricks."

www.ingramcontent.com/pod-product-compliance
Lightning Source LLC
Chambersburg PA
CBHW071532100726
47908CB00004B/1375